The Hockey Book

THE MITCHELL  BROTHERS SERIES

Other Books in the Mitchell Brothers Series:

#11

The Hockey Book

THE MITCHELL BROTHERS SERIES

Brian McFarlane

Fenn Publishing Company Ltd.
Bolton, Canada

THE HOCKEY BOOK
BOOK 11 IN THE MITCHELL BROTHERS SERIES
A Fenn Publishing Book / First Published in 2006

Copyright 2006 © Brian McFarlane

The content, opinion and subject matter contained herein is the written
expression of the author and does not reflect the opinion or ideology of the
publisher, or that of the publisher's representatives.

Fenn Publishing Company Ltd.
Bolton, Ontario, Canada

Distributed in Canada by H.B. Fenn and Company Ltd.
Bolton, Ontario, Canada, L7E 1W2
www.hbfenn.com

Library and Archives Canada Cataloguing in Publication

McFarlane, Brian, 1931-
        The hockey book / Brian McFarlane.

(The Mitchell Brothers series ; 11)
ISBN 1-55168-312-1

        I. Title. II. Series: McFarlane, Brian, 1931- Mitchell Brothers series ; 11.
PS8575.F37H63 2006   jC813'.54   C2006-901868-5

THE HOCKEY BOOK

NOTE FROM THE AUTHOR

Many years ago, I decided I would try to write a book—a hockey book. There were two reasons for this, I was curious to know if I *could* write a book and I wanted to prove to my father that I was *capable* of writing a book.

My father, Leslie McFarlane was an established Canadian author—he wrote the first 21 books in the famous Hardy Boys' series and he also had written several hockey books.

So I plunged in and wrote not one but two hockey books. One was *Clancy: The King's Story*. It was about the career of a Hall of Fame defenseman, King Clancy. The other was *Fifty Years of Hockey: A History of the NHL*.

Since then, I have written over 60 books. Among my favourites are the books in this series about the fictional Mitchell Brothers.

The Hockey Book is the story of two young men who set out in 1931 to fulfill their dreams of playing in the NHL—on a Stanley Cup winning team.

What makes *The Hockey Book* different is that Max Mitchell, who has always shown a flair for writing, is the storyteller. Encouraged by his dad and his brother Marty, Max tentatively embarks on an ambitious plan—to write a hockey book. As a first-time author, only Max knows if his heroes—Sniper Parmalee and Bunny Baker—will be successful in their quest for Stanley Cup glory.

Will Max himself be rewarded with a publishing contract for his efforts? The odds against either happening are long.

Hopefully, among my readers, there are ambitious young people who set their sights high, who are saying to themselves, "Someday, I will write a book or a poem. Paint a picture; compose a song. Someday I will play for the Stanley Cup or in the World Series."

If you establish your goals early in life, and work hard to achieve them, you may be amazed, over time, at how successful you may become.

Brian McFarlane

CHAPTER 1

FIRE AT THE ARENA

It was Marty who first heard the Indian River fire engine in the distance. He'd been at his desk, doing his homework, and had just opened the bedroom window to let in some fresh air.

"Max, come here!" he shouted. "Look! There's a big fire in town. I can see the flames. Wake up, Max!"

Max Mitchell, Marty's older brother, had fallen asleep on one of the twin beds; a copy of Robinson Crusoe spread open on his chest.

He awoke instantly and ran to Marty's side.

"Wow. It's a fire all right. A big one. Looks like it's over on Chestnut Street. Could it be...? Oh, no..."

"It's the arena!" Marty exclaimed. "Come on. We've got to get over there."

The brothers threw on their hockey jackets, raced downstairs and told their parents, who were busy preparing dinner, what they'd seen.

"We're going to run over there," Max said.

1

"No, we'll all go," Harry Mitchell decided in an instant. "Max, get the car started. Marty, grab your camera."

Mr. Mitchell was owner of the Indian River Review, the town's only newspaper.

"If it's the arena, this is a huge story," he stated, reaching for his coat. "It'll be on our front page tomorrow. Come on, Amy!"

"But my dinner," Amy Mitchell protested.

"Forget dinner." Mr. Mitchell threw her a jacket. "Put this on," he commanded. "Turn off the stove."

Minutes later, the Mitchell's new 1936 Buick was racing down Chestnut Street. Brakes squealed as Harry Mitchell pulled the car into the arena parking lot. The Mitchell family bolted from the car and groaned when they saw flames leaping from the roof of the arena and flying embers lighting up the sky.

"It's going to burn to the ground," wailed Max. "There goes our hockey season."

"The firemen are trying to save it," Marty said glumly. "But it may be too late. They're pumping tons of water on the flames. I've got to take some photos."

On weekends and after school, both Max and Marty helped their dad with the newspaper. Marty, 15, a goalie on the town's junior hockey team, often took photos that appeared in the Review.

Max, who was two years older than his brother and a versatile athlete, had developed some writing skills. He'd had several articles published in his father's paper. Someday, perhaps, he'd try writing a novel. Or a biography of some famous hockey player.

Now, with the arena on fire, he pulled a pad and pencil from his pocket and began taking notes and talking to witnesses.

Both teenagers stood close to the fire truck. Marty snapped several photo shots of the firemen battling the blaze.

"Anybody inside the arena when it caught fire?" Max asked a fireman manning a hose. "Anybody hurt?"

"A few girl figure skaters were in the rink. And the manager and a janitor. But we got them all out."

Max was a husky six-footer with a mop of blond hair. Marty was shorter by two inches and stockier. He had red brown hair.

Max circulated through the crowd, asking questions of the spectators.

"When did you first see the blaze? Who called in the alarm? Did anyone run from the building?"

He was trying to find out if the fire was started deliberately. Was it arson?

Marty snapped a shot of a burly fireman in an orange slicker when he turned to the crowd and hollered, "Get back! Stay back!"

That photo—the man's stern face, flames soaring in the background, was on the front page of the Review the following day.

Max then hurried to the side of the arena. He wanted to see if the dressing rooms were ablaze. Here the flames and smoke were less intense.

The wind blew a shower of sparks from the roof, where the fired raged out of control, to the back of the building, not far from where Max now stood. He was about to turn and go back when he noticed smoke pouring from a partially opened door.

Then he heard something over the whoosh of the wind and the roar of the fire. It sounded like a wail or the howl of a dog. And it was coming from inside the arena.

"My gosh, there's someone in there!" he murmured aloud.

Instinctively, Max started toward the half open door. The people at the front were focused on the flames that erupted from the roof.

Then his mother saw what Max planned to do.

"Max!" Amy Mitchell shrieked. "Come back! Don't go in there!"

But Max was already at the door, on his hands and knees to avoid the billowing smoke that poured from the opening.

"Is someone in there?" he shouted, peering into

4

the dark through stinging eyes.

A weak voice sobbed, "I'm here."

Max was frightened. He was tempted to scamper away, to seek help from the firemen. But that would take time—precious time—and there was no time to lose. Whoever had cried out from inside the building needed help—now!

Crawling on his hands and knees, Max pushed open the door, releasing another plume of smoke. He took a deep breath and held it. If he was going inside, he didn't dare inhale. He moved forward, reaching out with his right hand, extending it as far as he could. The floor was warm to his touch. He crawled a little deeper into the building and realized he would have to back out and take another deep breath. It was then he felt his hand brush against something soft. Hair! He clutched a thick mop of curly hair in his clenched fist and pulled on it. He felt a body slide toward him. His head began to pound and his need for fresh air was excruciating. But he refused to let go of the hair.

"Don't panic," he told himself, as he pulled harder. "Ease yourself back. Get out of here! Don't even think of taking a breath or you're a goner."

Max backed out through the doorway, almost in a panic and somehow stumbled outside. He gasped for breath, dizzy and disoriented. He eased the young person he'd pulled from the gymnasium to a place on the grass where the air was clean and fresh, pulling him away from the lethal smoke. Coughing and gulping fresh air into his tortured lungs, he lifted the unconscious youth in his strong arms and staggered away from the scene.

Then he heard his mother's voice. "Max! Max! I thought you were going to die in there." She ran to him and cried out, "Oh, no," when she saw the crumpled body in his arms.

"Is he...is he alive?"

"Yes, he's alive, Mom. I felt a pulse. He's one of the younger kids. His name is Billy Beemer. He swallowed some smoke. But he's breathing. Yes, he's alive."

"Thanks to you, son," she cried out. "Come on. Let's get him into an ambulance. You saved Billy's life."

At Merry Mabel's the next day, everyone was still talking about the fire. And how ten-year-old Billy Beemer almost died.

"The hockey season was just about to begin," wailed George McLeod, a junior hockey star. "Now we have nowhere to play. What rotten luck!"

Max's friend Trudy Reeves spoke up. "The figure skaters are just as unhappy," she said. "Indian River was going to host the North Country championships in March. My friend Elsie Whitt was a candidate for a medal. Now they'll move the finals somewhere else."

Max and Marty were sitting on stools at the counter. Max was reading the account of the fire he'd written for the Review while Marty was staring proudly at the front-page photo he'd taken of the fireman.

Max spun around on the stool and called for attention.

"Listen, gang, I know it's a disaster. But it could have been worse. Marty and I survived a fire in Haileybury not long ago. It wiped out the whole town. A lot of people died in that fire."

"Still, the arena was a big part of our community," George McLeod declared. "It may take years before we get another one. Our hockey season's ruined."

"Hey, wait a minute," Max responded. "I just came from Mayor Billing's office. I'm writing a follow-up story for the Review. The Mayor told me that the building is not a total loss. It will need a new roof and some extensive repairs to one dressing room and the front lobby. He figures in four months the old rink will be back in operation. That's not too long to wait."

Marty had more good news. "The Mayor told us the town would build an outdoor rink—where the ball park is. We may have to cut back on the number of games we play—but at least we'll be playing."

The kids began to cheer up. Much of the gloom in Merry Mabel's was dispersed.

Trudy had a question. "Is Billy Beemer still in the hospital, Max? Some kids blame him for the fire. They say he was playing with matches in one of the dressing rooms."

Trudy's comment drew a lot of chatter.

George said, "Wouldn't surprise me. That kid is weird. He was caught playing with matches before."

Max held up one hand. "We don't know that for sure. At the moment, Billy's not guilty of any-thing. There'll be an investigation. I'm going to the hospital right now to see how Billy's coming along."

Billy Beemer was happy to see Max. He wanted to thank him again for saving his life.

"No big deal, Billy," Max said. "You'd have done the same for me."

Billy offered a wan smile. "No, I couldn't have pulled you out. I'm not strong enough."

"Are you feeling better? Have they told you how long you're going to be in here?"

"I'm feeling better, Max. I swallowed a lot of smoke, I guess. I may be here a few days more."

"What happened? Why were you in the rink? What were you doing in there?"

"I went in to watch the figure skaters. They do

nice spins and things. Then I had to pee so I went into one of the empty dressing rooms."

Max leaned forward. "Were you playing with matches in there, Billy?"

"No, Max. My folks caught me playing with matches once—about a year ago—and grounded me. That was in our garage."

"You sure, Billy?"

"Yep."

Tears welled up in Billy's eyes.

"What's wrong, Billy?"

"Can you keep a secret, Max?"

"Sure."

"Well, the real reason I ran into the arena was to get away from my dad. He found out that I...that I wet the bed...again. He got mad and chased me out of the house. He'd been drinking. He's always drinking. He screamed at me and called me a big baby. He said I was useless and would never amount to anything."

"I'm so sorry, Billy."

Billy reached out and took Max by the hand. "You won't tell, will you? The kids at school tease me enough. About my name and things. If they knew about the bed wetting and my dad's drinking, they'd never let up."

"Kids can be cruel," Max said with a sigh. "Even if they don't mean to be. Remember, Billy, you're not the only one. Some of those kids are bed wetters, too. And some of them have parents who drink too much."

"I bet they don't feel as bad as I do."

Max sighed. "Billy, I don't know how I can help. I think you should talk to a professional person, like the school counsellor. Or a doctor."

"No, Max, I only want to talk to you. You can keep a secret. My dad will beat me if he finds out I told someone he's a...he's a drunk. And that I...you know... wet the bed."

Max hesitated before asking Billy another question. But he decided it was important.

"Billy, the other kids in the arena got out safely when the fire broke out. You could have, too. Is it because you didn't want to?"

Billy gave Max an anguished look. He nodded.

"I curled up on the dressing room floor," he cried. "I just wanted to go to sleep and never wake up. But when I started to choke, I changed my mind and crawled to where you found me."

Max was convinced that Billy Beemer needed professional help. But he'd promised not to tell. He'd have to think about what to do next.

When it was time to leave, he said, "Is there anything I can get you, Billy?"

Billy wiped his eyes and looked at the ceiling over his bed. Then he made a strange request.

"This may sound funny but I read all the articles you write for the paper. I think they're good.

Some are really good. Especially the ones about sports."

"Thanks, Billy. But what are you trying to say?"

"Well, I was just wondering if you'd write something just for me. A sports story maybe."

Max was surprised. "You mean something I'd make up?"

Billy's eyes focused on Max. "Yes. Maybe one about hockey."

Max smiled at Billy Beemer. "I've never written anything like that."

"But you could try, couldn't you?"

Max grinned. "Yes, I could try."

CHAPTER 2
THE OLD UNDERWOOD

Max Mitchell, a two-fingered typist, pecked away at his father's old Underwood typewriter. One round key—the letter P—balked when he tapped a finger on it. But the others appeared to be working fine.

Across the room, his brother Marty looked up from the Hardy Boys book he was reading. He eyed Max curiously.

"Did Dad give you that old thing?" he asked.

"Yep. He bought three new ones this week—one for his office at the Review, the other two for the reporting staff."

"Some staff," snorted Marty. "There's only old Charlie McNab full time. Mom does the obits and social news and takes care of the advertising. And you cover sports and other events part time. I get to take photographs once in a while."

Max shrugged. "I guess that's why Dad calls it a family business. Did you know he was thinking of raising the price of the paper from three cents to four?"

"I hope he knows what he'd doing," sighed Marty. "It's a lot to ask—four cents for a newspaper."

"Not for the *Review*, it's not," Max argued. "Dad turns out a great paper."

"You'd better learn to type with all fingers if you want to be a newspaperman," Marty said. "You're pretty slow."

"I'll get better," Max replied. "Say, this old typewriter sure makes a clacking sound. And the letter P isn't working very well. It sticks."

"Then use words without that letter," Marty suggested with a grin. "What are you writing, anyway?"

"A story."

"What kind of story?"

Max sighed. "It's nothing. Marty, I'm trying to concentrate," he said. "You mind?"

"I want to know," Marty persisted. "What kind of story?"

"It's just a hockey story. If you must know, I promised Billy Beemer I'd try to write a story for him."

"Really? Billy Beemer, huh? A hockey story?"

Marty was suddenly interested. He put down his book, crossed the room and hovered over Max, peering over his shoulder.

He began to read out loud. "From the drop of the puck, Sniper Parmalee sprang into action. He wheeled at centre ice and fired a pass to his winger. He took a return pass and barrelled into the two opposing defensemen. One staggered and fell. Sniper raced in between them. He drew back his stick and lashed a shot at…"

"Enough," Max said. "Go read your own book."

"But it's interesting," Marty responded. "Who the heck is Sniper Parmalee?"

"I told you it's a hockey story. He's one of the players. I made him up."

"Oh, yeah. Is he any good? Is he the hero?"

"Yes, he's the hero. Now let me get back to work."

"No, I want to read more." Marty noticed a pile of paper on the desk beside the typewriter. "You've written all that? You writing a whole book? When does this story take place?"

"Well, the story is turning out to be longer than I expected. It takes place in 1931—five years ago. It's what they call a novelette, I guess."

"You guess? Brother, I'm impressed. What are you going to do with it? Can you sell it?"

"Marty, stop asking so many questions, will you?" Max turned away from the typewriter. He got up and grabbed his brother by the elbow. "Come on," he said. "I need a break. Let's go down to Merry Mabel's for some ice cream. We'll ride our bikes."

At Merry Mabel's, they sat in a booth eating hot fudge sundaes. They had just been served when two high school friends—Trudy Reeves and Sandy Hope—came through the door. Marty waved them over.

A few weeks earlier, Max and Marty had rescued the two girls from a kidnapping. A pair of local youths, embarking on criminal careers, had stolen, among other things, a prized baseball from Sandy—one autographed by the famous Yankee slugger Babe Ruth, the home run king. When the girls discovered a shed outside of town where the thieves had stored their loot, they were captured by the young criminals, tied up and left in the woods. The Mitchell brothers rescued them, fought and subdued the thieves who were now serving time in prison.

"Two more sundaes, Mabel," Marty shouted across the restaurant. "And don't forget my brother's paying." Max merely rolled his eyes as the girls sat down.

"We'll pay," Trudy offered. "It's the least we can do to reward you two heroes—our rescuers. I still shudder when I think of those two thugs tying us up in the woods. They would have stolen Sandy's baseball and left us there if you hadn't come along."

"Those two are in prison for a stretch," Max said. "I hope they've learned their lesson."

"So what's new?" Sandy said, shaking her curls.

"Not much," Max replied. "Dad bought some new typewriters for the newspaper. And he gave me his old Underwood."

"Max has been pounding away at it," Marty said. "He's writing a book, a best seller. With two fingers. And he's not using a single word with the letter P in it."

"Come on, Marty. You weren't supposed to tell..."

"Are you really writing a book, Max?" Trudy asked, leaning forward. "Now that's interesting. What kind of best seller?"

"It's nothing," Max said, blushing. "Dad told me once I should try my hand at fiction, so with this old typewriter available, I thought..."

"But what kind of fiction?" Sandy asked.

"Hockey fiction," Marty said before Max could speak. "About a guy named Parmalee—Sniper Parmalee. And how he won the Stanley Cup in 1931."

"There's two P's right there—in Sniper's name," Sandy noted. "I thought you said..."

"The letter P works if you hit the key hard enough," Marty explained. "Anyway, this kid Sniper wins the Cup..."

Max struck his brother on the elbow. "You don't know that," he said sharply. "Even I don't know how the story will end." He smiled at Trudy and Sandy. "Anyway, why all this fuss over a hockey story that's probably not very good?"

"I'll bet it ends with Parmalee scoring the winning goal in the Stanley Cup," Marty insisted. "That's the kind of story I want to read."

"Do you have a publisher, Max?" Trudy asked.

Max grinned. "No, of course not. I thought I might send it in to one of the sports pulp magazines when it's finished. But only if Dad thinks it's good enough."

Trudy frowned. "What are pulp magazines?"

"Magazines printed on cheap paper. Mostly adventure stories and sports stories. They come out every month and sometimes the stories are printed in three or four installments."

Sandy said, "My parents read them. Dad buys Thrilling Sport Stories every month. They're only ten cents. And Mom reads love stories. True Love and Real Romance. Yuck!"

"Why are you writing about hockey in 1931?" Trudy asked.

"I guess it's because Maple Leaf Gardens opened in 1931," Max replied with a shrug. "And the Leafs won the Stanley Cup that season."

They finished their sundaes. The girls insisted on paying for themselves.

"Got time for a joke?" Marty asked before they left.

"Sure," Trudy said.

"Well, this farmer goes to prison and his wife has to look after the farm. But she's not very good at it. So she writes her husband and asks the best time to plant the potatoes. He writes back, 'Don't go near the potato field. That's where I buried all of my guns.' Of course, the prison officials censor the mail and a dozen cops rush to the farm and dig up the field looking for guns. So the farmer writes his wife another letter. 'You can plant the potatoes now.'"

Marty laughed at his own joke and slapped his thigh. The girls laughed politely too. Max just rolled his eyes.

Outside the restaurant, Max took Trudy aside. "There's a great new movie playing at the Bijou this week. It's called *Modern Times* starring Charlie Chaplin. Want to go see it with me?"

"Sure, Max. I'd love to. People say it's one of the best movies of 1936. What night?"

"Friday or Saturday."

"How about Saturday?"

"It's a date. I'll pick you up."

When the Mitchell brothers arrived back home, Marty complained of a headache.

"Must have been the ice cream," he told Max. "Think I'll go lie down for awhile."

In the room they shared, Marty went straight to the Underwood. He ran one hand over the keys. Then he picked up the manuscript Max had laid next to the typewriter.

"Hmm...that's a lot of pages," he murmured. "Max must have been working on this secretly for a long time."

Marty turned on the lamp beside his bed and adjusted the pillow. Then he lay down and began to read about Sniper Parmalee.

CHAPTER 3

UNCLE SIMON SAYS NO

A howling November snowstorm swept across the prairies.

In the kitchen of a rundown farmhouse, "Sniper" Jack Parmalee shuddered from a draft that filtered through the thin walls. He finished his nightly chores of washing the dishes and sweeping the unpainted pine boards that served as a floor. He pulled aside a thin curtain and looked out the window. Driven snow swirled past the dark pane of glass and the reflection showed his lean, sharp-eyed face.

"Will I be able to take the car into town tonight, Uncle Simon?"

Simon Parmalee, settled comfortably in his rocking chair close to the stove, put down his copy of the Farmer's Almanac and scowled. A gaunt, beetle-browed man with taught skin and a hard jaw, he was not an attractive specimen at the best of times. But when he scowled, he looked like an actor in a Hollywood horror movie.

20

"You out of your mind, boy?" he said harshly. "You see that storm out there? No, you can't have the car tonight. I'm not wasting money on gasoline for some fool hockey game."

Sniper—the nickname had been given to him by admiring teammates on the Wheatville hockey club as a tribute to his deadly shot—turned away with a grimace. He looked out the window again, and then asked, "Could I take one of the horses, then?"

"No!" shouted his uncle. "You can't have one of the horses, neither. It's not a fit night out there for man nor beast."

"But, Uncle Simon, the fellows are counting on me to be there tonight. It's an important game."

"Let 'em count," rasped Simon Parmalee. "And quit pesterin' me." He glared at his nephew over his magazine. "Hockey, hockey and more hockey. That's all I hear from you day and night. It's just a stupid game. Forget it. And be quiet!"

Sniper stared glumly out the window. Snow was piling up on the sill. He never disputed his uncle's authority; in fact, he seldom disputed anyone's authority. But lately, a few months shy of his eighteenth birthday, he had begun to realize that he was letting his sourpuss of an uncle treat him like a four-year-old.

He pulled back his shoulders and looked over at the hard-faced man in the rocking chair. His uncle was beginning to doze off.

"I suppose I could walk to town. It's not *that* far."

The old man's head shot up. He turned and glared at Sniper.

"Sure you could walk," he agreed. "It's only five miles over a frozen dirt road that's covered with drifts. It's a lovely night for a little stroll." He threw up his arms. "Listen, I don't want you to feel like a prisoner in my house. Be my guest. Walk into town. But don't be calling me in the middle of the night from one of my neighbours, begging me to come and get you. Walk if you want. You won't get far." He returned to his magazine.

Sniper stacked the dishes in the cupboard. He held a coffee cup in his big hand and squeezed hard. He was tall and slender but the muscles in his arms bulged under his flannel shirt. A combination of athletics and hard work on the farm had given him a strong upper body—a body that was still developing.

And he had stamina. As first-string centre on the Wheatville Wildcats he had often played the full sixty minutes of a game without relief.

Red Tilson, the Wildcats' coach, could scarcely believe Sniper's endurance. "He's the easiest player I've ever coached," he told his cronies. "He's a lot stronger than he looks. He seldom takes a penalty and he's got enough natural talent for half a dozen centres. And that shot of his..."

"He must have some faults," someone reminded him.

"Well, sure. He's not a happy kid. Doesn't laugh or joke around like most teenagers. Who knows why? Probably because of that crabby uncle he lives with—his guardian. And he never seems to fight back. He may lack a little backbone. But his skills more than make up for that. And he does what he's told."

There was no doubt that Sniper Parmalee would do what he was told. A dozen years serving his Uncle Simon had seen to that. It had been a dozen years of unquestioning obedience to a rigid, sometimes cruel caretaker.

Twelve years earlier, on a winter's night in 1919, five-year-old Jack Parmalee had been with his parents in the family car. They were on their way to visit relatives in a distant town. Jack was asleep on the back seat when the car skidded on ice while approaching a bridge. His father lost control and the car plunged into the ditch and splashed front first into the river. A trucker, approaching from the opposite direction, witnessed the accident and heard the screams. He jumped from his cab and raced to the scene, too late to rescue the Parmalee parents but just in time to snatch the child from the back seat. In moments, the car filled with water and disappeared, carried away by the strong current.

Although he was only five, Jack Parmalee would never forget the horror of that night. Or the funeral that followed. He wore his Toronto hockey jersey to the funeral—insisted on it. "Dad gave it to me for Christmas," he said, choking back tears. "He was teaching me how to play hockey. Told me I'd probably play in the NHL one day. He would have wanted me to wear it."

Nobody argued with the child. Only a handful of relatives and friends attended the brief service. And when it was over and the trip to the graveyard ended, Jack was led away—by his uncle Simon.

"I'm going to care for you, boy," his uncle told him. "Nobody else volunteered. I'll be your guardian until you're eighteen." He took Jack by the elbow and gave him a shake. "You'll do as I say. You won't give me any trouble, will you?"

The dazed boy shook his head. "No, Uncle Simon. I won't."

Simon squeezed his arm—hard. "Not if you know what's good for you, you won't." He smiled through crooked, tobacco-stained teeth. Jack Parmalee, already devastated and confused by the loss of loved ones, was thoroughly cowed.

"And you'll work hard for me, Jack. Farm life ain't easy. But it'll be good for you, you'll see. And you'll have a big brother. My son Butch will help take care of you."

Cousin Butch was 15, ten years older than Jack

and he resented having his cousin move in. He was a carbon copy of his father—mean, surly, cantankerous. Butch turned out to be more of a bully than a brother. He called Jack a "wimp" and a "weasel" and tormented him constantly. Whenever Uncle Simon was gone from the house, Butch ordered Jack to do all of the household chores. If Jack was slow to obey, Butch would pinch his arm or step on his toe with a heavy boot. "And if you squeal to my dad, I'll pick you up and throw you down the hole in the outhouse," he threatened. "Or drag you down to the creek and hold your head under water." Jack never squealed. The thought of being forced down that hole in the outhouse terrified him. Butch was strong enough to do it. Jack kept his lips sealed.

Jack soon realized that life wasn't pleasant for Butch, either. His father's rages when chores were left undone or unfinished, or when his son dared to question his strict orders, led to beatings with a razor strap or at the very least, a hard slap to the back of the head.

Jack worried that one day, when Butch grew up, he might turn on his father and beat him to a pulp.

In winter, Butch spent much of his spare time playing hockey. He was an awkward, mean-spirited defenseman on the Wheatville junior club who spent a good portion of every game in the penalty box. He possessed a hard, heavy shot, which he often drilled at a rival goalie's head.

"Scares 'em to death," he told Jack, chuckling. "Or it makes 'em mad. No matter. It throws them off and makes them easier to beat with your other shots. I'll teach you that shot if you'll shovel out the lane for me."

Jack was grateful when Butch taught him how to shoot a puck. Wearing their work boots, they practiced in the farmyard with the barn door serving as a backstop. But there was another price to be paid for Butch's daily instructions. Jack had to play goalie for Butch when his shooting lesson ended.

Butch dressed Jack in home made goalie gear— old cushions strapped to his legs and chest—an old catcher's mitt for a glove—and backed him up against the barn door. The next half hour became a matter of survival for Jack. He ducked and dodged an endless barrage of flying pucks aimed in his direction. He even stopped a few. Many of the shots were high, accompanied by a hoot of laughter from Butch when the pucks whistled over Jack's head and smacked into the barn door. It was a tribute to Jack's quick reflexes that he was never harmed by one, except for a few bruises. He was never cut or knocked unconscious.

One day Butch was shooting pucks particularly hard when the barn door flew open behind Jack.

Uncle Simon, hearing the racket, emerged from the barn in a snit.

"Stop that shooting!" he snarled, just as Butch unleashed a shot. The puck struck his father right in the jaw and staggered him. Blood oozed from a cut on his father's chin.

Dazed but furious, Simon Parmalee picked up the puck and hurled it at Butch, striking him on the knee. Then he ran into the barn, grabbed a horsewhip and came back out, wiping blood from his chin.

"I'm going to give you a good whipping, boy," he threatened. "You hit me deliberately."

"But I didn't," Butch protested, fear in his eyes. He'd suffered beatings from his dad for most of his life. Now he faced another one. He began to back off, and when his father raised the whip, he turned and ran. Butch raced into the house and up the stairs, his father in pursuit. He slammed and locked his bedroom door and hastily began throwing clothes into a suitcase.

By then, his father was pounding on the bedroom door.

"I'll horsewhip you good," he shouted, rattling the doorknob.

Trembling, Butch slammed the suitcase shut, snatched up a few dollars he'd saved and hidden in his underwear drawer, and stuffed the money in a pocket. He moved to the window, opened it and slipped through, stepping onto the porch roof. He scrambled down the roof, knocking shingles loose and dropped to the ground. He took off through the corn field, hurtled a fence at the end of it and when he reached the dirt road leading into town, he was breathing hard and perspiring freely. He slowed his pace but not by much. And he kept looking back.

"He won't beat the snot out of me never again," he mumbled to himself. "I'm off to be a hockey player."

With Butch gone, life on the farm was even more arduous for Jack Parmalee. Uncle Simon made certain of that. There were endless chores to tackle and complete—before and after school. The old farmhouse, with no insulation and a leaking roof, was frigid in winter and stifling in summer.

Jack had no toys to play with and no friends. There were no dogs or cats on the farm. Uncle Simon's nearest neighbour, Bill Bates, lived a mile down the road. They didn't talk much.

Jack wore the same pair of overalls every day— even to school. When he asked for regular clothes like the other kids, Uncle Simon laughed and said, "You don't need fancy duds for school. I wore overalls to school until I dropped out. You can, too."

"But they smell, Uncle Simon. I work in them

every day. Kids don't want to sit next to me on the school bus."

"It's a good farm smell," was the answer. "If you don't like it, wash them overalls in the river. Besides, them kids shouldn't be so snotty."

Jack learned how to wash his overalls. And his socks and underwear—not in the river but in a barrel of soapy water in the barn. One day, when he was hanging his wash out to dry, he found an old pair of skates stuffed in a second wooden barrel. There was other hockey equipment thrown on top—shin pads and gloves, half a dozen pucks and a pair of pants that were far too big for him. Next to the box was an old stick, heavily taped.

"Are they yours, Uncle Simon?" he asked, excited by his discovery. "Did you play hockey?"

"No, I never played hockey," his uncle answered. "It's a stupid game. Chasing' a piece of rubber with steel blades on your feet. It's nonsense. That stuff belonged to Butch." He picked up a skate and examined it. "What a waste of money."

Jack dared to ask a question. "Where did Butch go?"

"He ran off. That's all I know," Uncle Simon said bitterly. "He was worthless. Rebellious and pigheaded—just like his mother. She ran off too—a long time ago. I've no use for either one of them."

"And you don't know where they are?"

"Don't know, don't care. Butch may be a pro hockey player by now. He can't be very good. I've never seen his name in the papers. Course I don't read many papers."

"May I have his old skates, Uncle Simon? And his stick? My dad was a hockey player. He wanted me to be one too."

"Take the skates and stick. There's a patch of ice beside the barn. But don't expect me to shovel it off for you."

Jack Parmalee polished the skates. And sandpapered the rust off the blades. He found some leather laces in a pair of old work boots and worked them through the eyeholes of the skates. When he tried them on they were far too big. He knew they would be. Even when he pulled on several pairs of socks he still wobbled in the skates. But they would do.

He shovelled off the patch of ice and, when his chores were done, he hurried out to practice his skating. The moment his skates hit the ice his life on the farm became happier. He had something to look forward to each day.

That first winter he had no playmates and no coach. He stepped in ruts on the ice and fell down often. But he always got up. And he improved. And he told himself, *Jack, someday you'll be good. Good enough to play on a real team. Good enough to get away from Uncle Simon and this dumb farm.*

The side of the barn next to his patch of ice proved to be an inviting target. He thought of painting a bulls-eye on the barnboard—in red and white paint—but he feared his uncle's wrath. So he rolled the barrel in which he'd found the hockey gear to a place beside the barn and placed the open end facing his rink.

He began taking shots at the barrel opening. At first, he lobbed shots at the barrel and when that proved too easy he moved back a few paces. And he took harder shots. Before long he had the barrel jumping when his shots struck home. He'd shout, "Good save, barrel! Good save!"

He found another barrel and built a stand for the two barrels to rest on—about five feet off the ground. He pretended they were the upper corners of a hockey net.

His uncle watched him shooting pucks effortlessly into the barrels and it brought back memories. "Butch used to shoot high like that. He liked to make the goalies flinch. He'd shoot high and hard at them a few times, and then fool them with a low shot. He'd drive them goalies crazy. Drove me crazy, too. Always a troublemaker, that one. Good riddance to him."

Jack had memories of Butch, too. Not many of them were fond memories. Still, he had taught him how to shoot.

"He must have developed into a pretty good

player by now," he said to his uncle. "He may be the only pro player to come out of Wheatville."

"You think I care about that?" Uncle Simon said bitterly. "He deserted me. Said I was cruel and worked him too hard. I don't want to talk about him."

Jack went back to his puck shooting. *High shots*, he thought, *to make the goalie flinch. But they must be accurate shots. I'd never want to hit a goalie in the head.*

CHAPTER 4

A PLACE FOR SHINNY

One day in winter when Jack was fourteen, Uncle Simon went to town. Jack was on the rink when he heard someone call his name, "Hey, Jack!"

He looked up to see a farm boy on horseback waving at him. It was Elmer Bates, who lived on a farm down the road—a mile away. He'd seen Elmer on the school bus but had been too shy to speak.

"Hop on behind me," Elmer Bates shouted. "Hortense can carry two of us easily. We've got a real rink at my place. And four or five kids playing. We need another player."

"But I've got my skates on," Jack protested. "And my uncle will be mad if he comes home and I'm not here."

"So he gets mad. Come on! I'll get you back before you know it."

"But I can't ride behind you with my skates on."

"Sure you can," Elmer said, laughing. "I'll pull you up. And we'll use your skates as spurs if we have to. Old Hortense needs a little jolt every once in awhile to get her going."

Jack didn't need a second invitation. With Elmer's help he climbed up behind him. Hortense turned her neck and gave him a look before she started off through the field at her own steady pace. He didn't dare use his skates as spurs and was happy when Elmer didn't ask him to.

It was an afternoon Jack would never forget. He joined a happy band of kids roughly his own age in a prolonged game of shinny. Elmer Bates and his father had flooded a large area in their back-yard and placed low boards around the perimeter of their rink. Mr. Bates had even constructed hand-made goal nets for the players, the netting cut from a tennis net he'd purchased in town.

Jack noticed that one of the players was wearing a football-type helmet. On one rush, Elmer playfully shouldered the helmeted player into a snowbank. And the helmet flew off.

"Why, it's a girl!" Jack said in surprise. He went over to give her a hand. He pulled her upright. Blinded by the snow in her eyes, she blurted, "I'll get you back, Elmer. You did that on purpose." She swung her stick and hit Jack on the shins. "Ouch!" he said. She blinked several times, cleared her vision— and saw Jack.

"Oh, I'm sorry," she said. "I thought you were my brother. I didn't mean to..."

"I know, it's okay," Jack stammered.

The girl smiled at him and he felt something happen in his chest and in his head. She was beautiful. And he was almost speechless.

She said, "My name's Brenda. I'm Elmer's sister."

He bent to rub his bruised shin. "And I'm Jack. Jack Parmalee."

She smiled again. "Nice to meet you, Jack. I've seen you around at school."

"I've seen you too. You sing in the choir and I hear you get straight A's."

"Come on, play hockey!" Elmer interrupted. "Talk later."

Jack was the star of the scrambly game. He was much faster and more confident on his skates than the others. And his shot...!

The other boys were amazed when he unleashed a shot at the empty net. The puck ripped right through the strands of tennis net, skimmed over a snowbank and crashed through a small window in the Bates' garage.

"Oh, gosh!" cried Jack. "I'm sorry. I didn't mean to do that."

"Holy cow!" exclaimed Elmer. "I've never seen a kid shoot that hard. You're a real sniper."

Mr. Bates heard the sound of breaking glass and came charging out of the house. Jack was tempted to flee.

But Mr. Bates was laughing. He examined the hole in the netting and shook his head.

"That was some shot, Jack," he said admiringly. "I've taken a hundred shots at this net and never put one through. You must have been practicing."

"Yes, sir," Jack said. "Every day. I'm really sorry about the window. And the net."

"Forget about it," said Mr. Bates. "I can fix 'em both by tomorrow." He turned to the other boys. "Sun's going down, fellows. That's enough for today. Will you come back tomorrow, Jack?"

"I'd sure like to, Mr. Bates. But Uncle Simon..."

"I know, I know. He keeps you under a tight rein. Let me talk to him. Come on, I'll give you a ride back to the farm."

"I'm coming too, Dad." Brenda said.

"Where in tarnation have you been, you sneak?" Uncle Simon exploded when Mr. Bates drove Jack back to the Parmalee farm. "You ran off without permission."

Uncle Simon brandished a razor strap that Jack had seen—and felt—often in the past. He cringed and couldn't speak. And he was terribly embarrassed to have Brenda witness this scene.

Mr. Bates put up both hands. "We surrender, Simon," he said, smiling uneasily. "No need to punish the lad. He was invited to our place to play hockey. He's some player, I tell you. And that shot of his..."

"I'll give him a shot," Simon said coldly. "I hate

36

it when people run away on me. Well, it won't happen again."

"Come on, Simon. Be reasonable. The boys want Jack to come back. Tomorrow, in fact. And as often as possible."

"That'll be the frosty Friday," Simon snorted. "No way. Jack's grounded."

Brenda turned her back and walked away. A wave of pity for Jack swept over her. Tears had begun to well in her eyes.

"Have it your way, Simon," Mr. Bates replied with a smile. "But remember, when you want to borrow my manure spreader or my post hole digger again—like you do every year—I'm afraid the answer is no."

"You'd do that to me—your neighbour?"

"I would, Simon. Because you're being unreasonable. Jack needs to have fun. He needs the company of other young men. He works his butt off for you. Cut him some slack."

Simon Parmalee was torn. Bill Bates had never hesitated to lend him his farm machinery. Most neighbours would have told him no way, and one had even said this to his face, "Why not buy your own, you old skinflint." But Bill Bates had always been willing to share.

He put down the strap.

"I ain't got a choice," he said. "Jack, you can play with the boys on the Bates' rink."

In the car, Brenda turned to her father. "Poor Jack," she said quietly. "How awful that he's forced to live with such a...such a creature."

CHAPTER 5

GETTING TO THE GAME

Since that game of shinny—and many more that followed—on the Bates' frozen pond, Jack had become the star of the Wheatville junior team. And the nickname Elmer had given him stuck. Everyone knew him as Sniper Parmalee.

Jack sighed and turned away from the window.

"Guess I'll walk into town then," he said softly.

"Don't be a fool!" his uncle snorted. But permission had not been denied.

Jack looked at the clock on the wall. It was almost six o'clock. Game started at eight. Wheatville would meet Coyote Bluff in the first game of the season. He'd have to hurry.

Jack pulled on his heavy work boots. He slipped into his sheepskin coat, found a pair of thick mitts and yanked his fur hat down around his ears. He picked up his skates, which lay by the stove. The rest of his equipment was stored in a locker at the rink. But he carried his skates everywhere.

"Only an idiot would walk into town on a night

like this," his uncle growled.

"Seeing I can't have the car or one of the horses..."

For a breathless moment, he thought his uncle was going to relent, was going to understand how important the game was to Jack. But Simon Parmalee was a hard, bitter man. He had never recovered from the shock of his own son's sudden departure, how he'd bolted from his home to follow his hockey dreams. The very word hockey was enough to make him bristle with anger.

"Walk then, you little bugger," he growled vindictively. "You'll get a mile down the road and head back. Don't count on the door being unlocked."

He settled back in his chair and glared at Jack. "Hockey! Wish I could get hold of the fellow who invented that game. I'd tell him a thing or two."

"See you, Uncle Simon," Jack said meekly. "I may stay in town tonight with one of the fellows. But I'll be back in time for milking in the morning."

"You better be. Now get out of here!"

There was contempt in the raspy voice of Simon Parmalee, the contempt of the bossy man for one who allows himself to be bossed too easily.

Sniper let himself out the back door. A blast of icy wind whipped around the corner of the woodshed and struck his face, bringing tears to his eyes. He trudged through the drifts, head down, toward the lane. Near the barn he hesitated. Inside was the old Ford, keys on the dash where his uncle always left them. The car would get him to town in a few minutes, providing the drifts weren't too high. The car was reliable in snow. And the heater worked well.

Then he shook his head morosely. His uncle had said "No" and his uncle's word was law. At least on the farm.

Jack sighed and hurried down the lane. He didn't want to be late.

Red Tilson, coach of the Wheatville Wildcats, held up the start of the hockey game as long as he could.

"Terrible weather," he told the referee. "My boys had to scramble to get here. They're still getting dressed."

"Coyote Bluff got here in time," the ref replied. "And they had to travel twenty miles. I'll give you another ten minutes but no more."

After ten minutes there was a pounding on the dressing room door. "Come on, Tilson. Get yer team on the ice."

Tilson took one more look at his watch. The Wildcats would have to face the visitors without their top scorer—Sniper Parmalee.

"Let's go, boys! Let's go!" he shouted.

"You'll have to take Sniper's place until he shows up," the coach told George Hammel, second-line centre, patting him on the back. He turned to Harry Hogan, a volunteer fireman in town and the team trainer. "You tried to phone him, didn't you?"

"Yep. I called the Parmalee farm. Old Simon said Sniper had left for town. I think I woke the old man up. He hung up on me before I could ask him when the young fellow started out."

"He's a nasty old buzzard," Tilson sighed. "I'll bet Sniper had a tough time getting the car keys from him. Maybe he got stalled in a snowdrift. Why don't you take my truck and head out that way. Maybe that old Ford is stuck in a drift somewhere."

"Sure," said Hogan and ducked out of the dressing room.

Tilson went out and crossed the ice to the Wheatville players' bench. He received a polite round of applause from the fans who, despite the foul weather, jammed the shabby little rink. Even indoors, the temperature was well below freezing. But the fans didn't seem to mind. The anticipation, the excitement of a rousing hockey game can be as warming as a bonfire.

Twenty miles of flat road separated the two prairie towns, each with a population of about three thousand. Their residents mixed and mingled at fall fairs, cattle auctions and other events. Generally, they got along. But during hockey season, the rivalry between the towns was fierce.

Tilson studied the Coyote Bluff players warming up at one end of the rink. He noted that some of them were wearing earmuffs, not only to guard against frostbite but also to tune out the insults hurled at them by the Wheatville fans. He was particularly interested in the padded figure tending the visitors' goal. He had been told that Coyote Bluff was introducing a new goaltender—a fellow named Baker—and he was reputed to be a sensational puckstopper.

"We'll see," Tilson muttered to himself. "The newcomer may have an easy night of it if Sniper doesn't show up. If he does, well, I've never seen a goalie yet who can stop Sniper."

Tilson watched the padded figure nonchalantly kicking out and batting aside shots fired at him by the Bluff players and was impressed.

"Bunny" Baker, in the Bluff net, was a sturdy, round faced young man whose girth was emphasized by his playing gear. He wore a peaked cap at a jaunty angle and chewed on four sticks of gum, which bulged in one cheek. He looked cool and calm, not at all concerned. A flip of his stick, an outstretched foot, an upflung arm, an easy slide across the crease. He didn't appear to exert himself and he always managed to stop the puck.

Tilson knew hockey. And he recognized talent when he saw it. He knew that economy of effort is the hallmark of a true goalie. "Come on, Sniper," he murmured. "Get here. We're going to need you tonight more than ever."

CHAPTER 6

The players lined up along the blue lines. The Wheatville High School band played the national anthem. The referee dropped the puck and the annual winter hockey feud was underway.

George Hammel won the draw and flipped the puck across to Denny on left wing. Denny dodged around his check, darted in and fired a hard shot from inside the blueline.

Coyote Bluff's new goaltender barely moved. He picked the shot out of the air with his glove, dropped it to his stick and snapped it out to Ferguson, his big centreman.

Denny wheeled and started back but he was caught up ice.

Ferguson hustled down the unguarded lane. His rush was stopped at the Wheatville blueline.

The game was underway in earnest and still no sign of Sniper Parmalee.

Hammel was an eager, hard-working player. But he lacked speed and his checking was questionable. In the first two minutes, Ferguson pulled away from him twice. Using his size, Ferguson waded through the Wheatville defenders and pulled Gus Gagnon out of his net, scoring easily. First goal of the new season.

Tilson changed lines and his second stringers surprised him. They managed five straight shots on goal. Against an average netminder they might have tied the score or even pulled in front. But this man Baker was no run of the mill goalie. He handled the shots with ease, constantly moving his wad of gum from cheek to cheek.

Then Wheatville got a break. A Coyote Bluff defenseman pulled down an incoming forward and was thumbed to the penalty box. The hometown fans roared their approval. Tilson sent out his starting line.

The faceoff was inside the Bluff zone. Hammel snared the puck when it hit the ice and whipped a pass over to Denny. Denny eluded a check and ripped a shot on goal.

Apple-cheeked Bunny Baker moved quickly to block it but he couldn't smother the rebound. Hammel collared the bounding puck and drilled it hard for the upper corner. Somehow, Baker got his glove up just in time. He deflected the puck over the crossbar. Denny tore in after it, pulled it out in front and tried to slip it inside the post. No luck. Baker's foot was there to block it.

Hammel came racing in to help. He snared the loose puck and shot it toward the far corner. But Baker's other big boot shot out and turned it aside.

"Doggone it," groaned Hammel in frustration as a Bluff defender crosschecked him into the ice. The referee blew his whistle and Coyote Bluff drew another penalty.

Tilson breathed easier. His team enjoyed a two-man advantage. Wheatville couldn't help but score now.

But Baker was just getting warmed up. The Coyote Bluff goaltender began to take a real interest in proceedings. He chewed harder on his gum. He tugged at the peak of his cap and crouched lower in his net.

Then he went into action as the home team peppered him with shots.

Denny took the first one. From the faceoff, he snapped up the puck, took a stride and let go. Baker had pulled over a few inches, giving him an opening. Then, quick as lightning, he shifted back to make the stop. He steered the puck behind the net and winked at Denny as he flew past.

A Bluff defender tried to loft the puck down the ice but Hammel batted it down, wheeled and whipped a blistering shot at Baker. The newcomer deflected it with his skate. Wheatville right-winger Bert Morgan raced in for the rebound, fought for it and got a shot away. Baker did the splits, smothered the puck and fell on it. Smiling, he scrambled to his feet and flipped the puck to the referee.

At the Wheatville bench, Tilson shook his head in disbelief. "That guy doesn't belong in small town hockey," he said admiringly. "He's one of the best I've ever seen."

Moments later, at full strength, Coyote Bluff fans in the crowd had something to cheer about. Ferguson, their top threat, had scored again.

"Ouch!" groaned Tilson. "If Parmalee doesn't get here soon, we don't have a chance."

The hometown club tried everything in the book. Long shots, close in shots, shots high and low. It didn't matter. Baker gobbled them up as if they all looked alike. In their eagerness to score, the Wheatville boys neglected their checking. And Coyote Bluff scored three more goals. When the period ended, the hometown fans were in shock. Coyote Bluff 5, Wheatville 0. With two more periods to come.

In the dressing room, Gus Gagnon had words of praise for his counterpart.

"That fellow, whoever he is, is real good. He's got class. Wonder how he wound up in Coyote Bluff."

"I hear he's not going to be with Coyote Bluff for long," someone said. "He's headed east. Thinks he's good enough to try out with a pro team. Toronto, I think. This will be his first and last game against us."

"That's great news," Tilson declared. "We don't want to see him again. I sure wish one of you fellows would find a way to put a puck past him tonight. If only Sniper was here..."

The dressing room door shot open. Harry Hogan and Sniper Parmalee plunged into the room. Their faces were red, their jackets and hats covered with snow. Sniper was shivering, so cold he couldn't speak. But he struggled out of his coat before he was well over the threshold.

"He was walking!" Hogan yelped. "Can you believe it? Walking to town on a night like this. I picked him up a couple of miles out. Then we had trouble getting back. The car stalled twice trying to break through the drifts."

"You walked!" Tilson shouted. "In this kind of weather. How come?"

"Couldn't get the car," Sniper grunted. He had his mitts off and was unlacing his boots with stiff fingers.

"Why didn't you phone me? I'd have gone out and picked you up."

"Didn't want to bother anyone, coach. Besides, I'd have made it easy if I'd started earlier. But the storm got worse and the drifts were pretty deep."

"So you walked," Tilson snorted as he handed

Sniper pieces of his equipment. "Lucky you didn't freeze to death. You telling me your uncle wouldn't lend you the car on a night like this?"

Sniper shrugged. "You know my uncle. What's the score, anyway?"

"Coyote Bluff is leading 5-0. They've got a fellow in goal who looks like the ghost of Georges Vezina."

"Gosh! Five to nothing, eh? Guess we'd better pull up our socks. We can't let this new fellow shut us out."

CHAPTER 7

SNIPER MEETS BAKER

The Wheatville fans felt a little more optimistic when Sniper Parmalee took his place at centre for the start of the second period. They were well aware that he was the scoring star of the team. But they also recognized that the goalie for Coyote Bluff was a sensation, a little too polished perhaps for any of the Wheatville regulars.

Sniper had two good scoring chances in the opening minutes, taking a pair of wicked shots that Bunny Baker stopped as nonchalantly as if they were tennis lobs. The Wheatville fans groaned and began to give up hope.

At the seven-minute mark, Sniper stepped into a Bluff puck carrier at centre ice, knocking him flat. He snapped up the puck and wheeled over the blue line. From inside the line he pulled the trigger on a shot that rocketed toward Baker. It almost knocked his cap off before it hit the crossbar and sailed into the chicken wire behind his cage. Baker blinked and gave Sniper a second look.

Sniper swooped in after the puck and whipped a pass out to Denny who shot from close in. Baker kicked it aside.

A Bluff defenseman tried to clear the puck out of the zone. But Sniper alertly intercepted it and twisted around for another shot. Again it was high. Baker ducked as the puck whipped past his right ear.

For the next few minutes, there were few good scoring chances. Then the crowd roared as Sniper expertly hook checked the puck from under an opponent's stick and raced away with it.

Baker was nervous now. After those two hair raising shots, he didn't know what to expect. He saw Parmalee eye the top bar as he let fly. Instinctively, Baker ducked, but this shot was low, right along the ice. It slammed into the lower corner, bounced up and got caught in the mesh, then spun to the ice.

At last, the Wheatville fans had something to applaud. They rose as one man and howled with joy.

"There goes the new fellow's shutout," Red Tilson bellowed in Harry Hogan's ear. "I knew Sniper would find a way to beat him."

Bunny Baker slapped his goal stick on the ice. He was angry and he was puzzled; angry because of those high head shots that threatened to scalp him, puzzled because he'd been beaten by a shooter who'd shot low while apparently aiming high.

Sniper's goal gave his team a big lift while the Coyote Bluff forwards lost a bit of their confidence. And Gus Gagnon promptly thwarted two of their solo efforts. On the second one, he propelled the puck up ice to Sniper, who was cruising inside the blue line.

Sniper raced away. He dodged a checker and found himself in the clear. Baker fell into his crouch and moved out to cut down the shooting angles.

Sniper tore in and faked a shot. Baker didn't move. Suddenly, Sniper cut sharply across the front of Baker's crease and backhanded the puck under Baker's outflung arm. The red light flashed again.

For a second time, Wheatville fans rejoiced noisily.

Bunny Baker looked puzzled. He had stopped many a backhand shot in his time. But that was the trickiest one that had ever beaten him.

He began to have a new respect for the late arriving centreman. The kid didn't belong in this small town brand of amateur hockey—not by a long shot.

From then on, the game became a battle between a master goalie and a determined scorer. They dominated the play. The other players, awkward and willing, were just cluttering up the ice.

Goalie Baker vowed he'd protect his team's

three-goal lead and Sniper Parmalee was just as determined to whittle that lead away.

Run of the mill shots from Parmalee's team-mates Baker handled easily. But those sharp, wicked drives off Parmalee's stick took him by surprise. They were burning with speed.

Down came the pesky centre again, scooting in over the blue line, swerving, cutting in fast, legs churning. Bunny Baker fell into his crouch. No corn-fed kid was going to make a fool of him.

Then he ducked frantically as a puck came from nowhere, straight for his head. It whizzed past and rattled into the screen where it stuck, wedged between strands of wire. The whistle blew.

Baker was irate. He stormed out of his cage. "Hey, listen you!" he raged, pointing his stick at Sniper. "What you trying to do? Knock my head off?"

Sniper swung around. "You talking to me?" he asked in a mild voice.

"Yeah, I'm talking to you, wise guy. You keep those shots down or I'll take a slap at you with this war club." He brandished the stick. "You're trying to bean me."

Sniper shook his head. "Gosh, no. Not really. I'm just trying to make you duck."

"Well, I'll make you duck in about two seconds."

"They're not really aimed at your head," Sniper assured the gum-chewing goalie. "It may look like it but they're just a bit higher. I'd never try for your head."

"You telling me you can call your shots that close," snapped Baker. "Impossible!"

"But I can. I've practiced for hours and hours. Next time don't duck. The puck will go about two inches over your head."

"You're crazy, kid," growled Baker. He shook his head and swung back into his cage.

Baker was still fuming after the exchange with the mild-mannered Parmalee. The kid had tried to make him believe six ounces of hard rubber sizzling straight for his head wasn't a threat to send him to the nearest hospital.

But fear had never been part of Baker's make-up—apprehension maybe—but not fear. And he wasn't about to let a slim farm boy make him shy away from flying pucks now.

"O.K. brother," he muttered. "Next time you try that, I won't duck. And if you hit me, I'll carve you into little pieces—as soon as I'm conscious."

For the next few minutes, the Coyote Bluff defense stiffened. Then Sniper snared a loose puck, squirted free of a defenseman's grasp and let drive. Baker flung up a glove to protect his face for the shot was high. Despite his vow not to duck, he ducked. The puck flew into the screen, then dropped to the ice. Denny and a defenseman raced in after it. The defenseman tried to pass it out to an uncovered wing. Sniper's stick flashed out. He intercepted it, headed straight for Baker. He swerved in front of the goal crease, held his shot, sped across the crease. This time Baker thought he had solved that backhand. He lunged. But the shot never came. Instead, Sniper showed him some sleight of hand with stick and puck and eased the puck just over the line inside the goal post. Baker blinked, unable to believe he'd been fooled again.

But there lay the puck in his cage. There was Sniper skating away. There was the red light. There was Baker, caught out of position.

The buzzer sounded. The period was over.

Bunny Baker scrambled to his feet, shaking his head.

"You're good, kid," he murmured to himself. "Real good. I'd rather have you playing with me than against me."

That gave Bunny an idea. He'd played goal against many a smart forward. And he knew a natural goal scorer when he saw one.

In the final period, two goals proved to be too great a margin for Wheatville to overcome although Sniper beat Baker once more with a low shot to the corner of the net. Coyote Bluff won the game by a 5-4 score.

Sniper's superb play at centre was taken for granted by the Wheatville fans. They had seen his scoring skills many a time and his four goals came as no surprise. But they'd seldom seen masterful goaltending like Baker displayed. He was regarded as a sensation.

The players mingled in the arena lobby after the game. The Coyote Bluff manager was busy on the phone attempting to make hotel arrangements. Because of the storm, the visitors would not be traveling back home tonight.

Bunny Baker was at the snack bar munching on a hot dog when he spotted Sniper across the lobby.

"Hey, kid, come over here for a minute."

When Sniper approached, Baker threw out his hand. "You played a solid game tonight, kid. Not often a kid your age beats me four times in a game. And in just two periods. I was working on a shutout until you came in from the storm. We were lucky to hang on for the win."

"You weren't lucky," Sniper told him. "You were great. You're the best goalie I've ever played against."

"And you've got the best backhand shot I've ever seen," said Baker. "I figured you for a high shot and you put it past me low. I play it low and it comes in high. How old are you, anyway?"

"Seventeen. Almost eighteen."

"Almost as old as me. But you look younger. And you look hungry. You gonna have a hot dog?

A drink?"

"No. I'm not hungry," Sniper stammered. "Besides, I don't have...well, I don't have any money."

"Treat's on me. You earned it."

They munched on hot dogs, wiped mustard from their mouths.

His mouth full, Bunny said, "Listen pal, do me a favour, will you?"

"Sure."

"Come down to the rink early tomorrow morning. I'm heading east, see. I hope to catch on with a pro club. But you showed me a few tricks with the puck tonight. I want to see if I can figure out that backhand of yours. Will you give me a workout in the morning. Won't take long."

Sniper paused. "Gosh, I'd like to. But I live on a farm out of town. I've got to be back in time for the milking tomorrow morning."

"Tell you what. We can work out real early and I'll drive you back to the farm. I'll even help out with the milking."

Sniper thought of his uncle's wrath. Then he thought of the kick he'd get out of practicing with a goalie who was almost certain to be in the NHL one day soon. Hockey was his one passion in life. Nothing else would have tempted him to risk Uncle Simon's fierce temper.

"I'd like to help, but..."

"That's great!" declared the goaltender as he paused to sign autographs for a pair of Wheatville fans. "I'll call the hotel. I'll make sure they put an extra bed in my room. And I promise to get you back home early—after the roads have been plowed. Then you can teach me how to get milk out of those thingamajigs on the cow."

"I'll catch it from my uncle," said Sniper, weakening. "There's just the two of us and…"

"Your uncle! What kind of old bird is he? What's his problem? You'd think he'd want you to stay in town tonight. Forget him."

"Nobody who meets my uncle ever forgets him," Sniper declared. "You don't know him."

"Don't want to know him either," Baker stated. "Sounds to me like he's an old tyrant. Come on, let's go. You look hungry. I'll buy you dinner at the hotel."

CHAPTER 8

A DECISION TO LEAVE

After milk shakes and a hot spaghetti dinner, Sniper wiped sauce from his shirt with a napkin and said, "You're a lot friendlier than I thought you'd be, Bunny. I figured you'd still be mad at me for taking those high shots at you."

Bunny Baker laughed. "Mad? I admit you got my goat with those bullets you fired over my head. But you shouldn't have backed down when I bawled you out. Why didn't you tell me to go fly a kite? It's your job to score goals. It's my job to keep 'em out."

"No, I've been thinking maybe I shouldn't be trying to frighten goalies with those high shots. My cousin Butch came up with that idea and Coach Tilson told me to do it. There's not much danger, really, because I aim them just high enough to miss."

"You mean you've got that much control?" sputtered the goalie.

"Yep. I can usually put the puck where I want it. That's from a lot of practice. On the farm, I learned how to lift the puck into barrels. And then into an empty paint can I nailed on top of the barnyard fence. I don't miss too often but then it's a pretty big can."

"With the shot and the smarts you showed me tonight, you ought to be in pro hockey, kid."

"Oh, I don't know," Sniper replied, blushing. "Uncle Simon says I wouldn't even get a tryout with a real hockey team. He says..."

"You Uncle Simon is full of cow manure," declared Bunny, slapping a big hand on the table. "Where do you think big league hockey players come from? Farms, villages, small towns. Every once in a while a kid comes out of nowhere to skate right to the top. You might be one of those guys. And I will be, too."

"I'm sure you will, Bunny. But as for me, well, there's a lot of difference between hockey in Wheatville and hockey in the big cities."

"Not as much as you think."

"And besides, Uncle Simon wouldn't let me go. My parents are dead and he's my guardian. His son Butch—my cousin—ran away to be a hockey player a few years ago and my uncle almost had a fit. Anyway, he needs me on the farm."

"Oh, sure. Cheap labour. You like working on the farm, Sniper?"

"No. Not really."

"Do you like playing hockey?"

"Love it. Best game in the world."

"Well, all I can say is any uncle who'll make a farm hand out of a natural born hockey player isn't worth paying much attention to. However, it's none of my business. Let's get some sleep. We'll have some fun in the morning."

Sniper wheeled at centre ice and struck out toward the net, increasing his speed with every stride. Bunny Baker, gripping his goal stick, crouched between the pipes, his eyes riveted on the puck on the blade of Sniper's stick.

In he came, skates flashing. Bunny pulled over, leaving an opening. Sniper grinned and refused to go for it. He knew Bunny would cover it in one swift lunge. He sped in close, faked a shot. Bunny didn't budge. Then, throwing up a shower of ice, Sniper cut across the crease and let fly with his backhand. Bunny darted over, threw out his glove. But the puck hit a goal post and caromed into the cage.

"Doggone it," Bunny said, exasperated. "I thought I had that one figured out. I thought you telegraphed it when you showed me that little lift of your shoulder. But you crossed me up."

Sniper swung back and stopped. He tried hard not to look too pleased with himself. "I saw you give me some room low on your stick side. So I banged it high over your glove. Almost missed, though."

Baker fished the puck out of the net. "That time I watched your wrists. But you got the puck away so fast. How do you do that?"

"Heck, I don't know," Sniper shrugged. "Lots of practice I guess. My wrists are pretty strong."

It was eight o'clock in the morning and they were the only occupants in the Wheatville rink.

"Listen, pal," said Bunny, leaning against the crossbar. "You've got one of the hardest and fastest shots I've ever seen. And I've seen plenty. Don't tell me you got it from pitching hay. No wonder they call you Sniper. And Uncle Simon is making a farmhand out of you. What a waste of talent."

Sniper grinned, took the puck and went back to work. He flashed in on goal for several more tricky, hard driven shots that tested Bunny's speed and sharpness of eye to the limit. Bunny made plenty of saves.

Sniper stopped again, breathing hard and told Bunny he was the best goalie he'd ever seen.

"And this is the best workout I've had in years," Bunny replied. "I learned a lot from you this morning. Well, let's call it a day. I promised to get you home and I will."

On the drive back to the Parmalee farm, Bunny said earnestly, "Look, Sniper, here's an idea. Why not come east with me and take a crack at pro hockey? You're wasting your time on the farm. If I didn't think you were good enough, I'd never suggest it. But you're plenty good, much better than you think."

The idea sounded so far-fetched that Sniper laughed. "It's nice of you to say so, Bunny, but...well, I don't think so. Maybe in a year or two."

"Now listen to me! I've been playing amateur hockey all my life. Played on junior teams that never got anywhere. So my goals-against-average has never looked good. But I know I'm a goalie and better than most. Last year a scout from the Leafs told me to come east any time I wanted a tryout. So I'm going. I don't want to be stuck in Coyote Bluff for the winter."

"The Leafs! Why, that's the team my cousin plays for—Uncle Simon's son, Butch Parmalee. He kicked around the minor leagues for years. Came up two seasons ago."

"Sure. I've heard of Butch Parmalee. Led the league in penalties. Meanest man in hockey."

"That's my cousin."

Bunny whistled. "He's a nasty one. Takes after his old man, I guess. Why the heck haven't you asked him to get you a tryout?"

"I haven't talked to him since he left the farm. Besides, he never liked me very much. He hasn't written or called since he left. But I can't just leave, Bunny. Uncle Simon has looked after me since my folks died. He's my guardian until I turn eighteen next year."

"Sounds like you're afraid of him. And afraid to strike out on your own."

"Sure I am. He'll chew my ear off for not getting back earlier. You'll see."

"Let me handle him," Bunny grunted.

They drove on in silence for a few minutes. Then Sniper said, "If you don't mind me asking, where'd you get the nickname Bunny?"

"When I first started playing goal someone said, 'Why, he's quick as a bunny and just as cute.' "

CHAPTER 9

A FIGHT ON THE FARM

They followed a snowplow almost all of the way to the farm. Bunny's old car made it easily. But when he pulled into the driveway, Uncle Simon emerged from the barn, carrying a snow shovel. His face was dark as a thundercloud.

"So you're back home at last!" he snarled. "Well, get to work! I'll punish you later."

"Sorry I'm late, Uncle Simon, you see…"

"I don't want to hear any of your excuses. I said get to work."

Simon Parmalee was a big man. He towered over his nephew. He hadn't shaved for several days, Bunny noted.

"Or bathed either," Bunny said to himself, sniffing the air when Simon moved closer. "He's about the nastiest looking old coot I've ever seen. No wonder Sniper is afraid of him."

Simon's tirade wasn't over. He turned on Sniper. "You said you'd be back for the milkin' and here it is the middle of the day. I guess that ends hockey for you."

"But it's just a little after ten," Sniper protested meekly.

"Shut up! Change your clothes and get to work! Start shovellin'."

"Hey, Mr. Parmalee," Bunny said. "It was all my fault. I talked Sniper into staying in town last night. I'm a goalie and I wanted to practice against him. The roads were so bad from the storm..."

"Bad roads, nothin'," snapped the uncle. "If he was able to walk to town he was able to walk back. I suppose you're another of them ignorant hockey players. Well, get that car off my property. Don't show your sorry face around here again."

Sniper said, "I'm sorry, Bunny. It was good of you to drive me home. Guess we better say goodbye."

Bunny leaned against the hood of the car. He chuckled.

"Sniper," he said calmly, "looks to me as if this old clump of cow dung has the hex on you. If you won't stand up to him, I'll do it for you." Cockily, he sauntered over to Simon.

"Listen, mister, what's the big idea treating a grown man like he was a little devil. Who do you think you are, you old goat?"

"One thing I am is the owner of this farm," Uncle Simon rasped, "and you're trespassing."

"So? What you gonna do about it?" Bunny turned to Sniper. "How much does this ugly uncle of yours pay you?"

The question surprised Sniper. "Why, nothing. I get room and board. And some clothes once in awhile."

Bunny put a hand on Sniper's shoulder. "Listen to me, pal. I like you a lot but I can see you don't have much backbone. Do you like your life out here?"

"I hate it."

"Look here!" his uncle bellowed, shaking a fist at Bunny. "Get out of here or I'll thrash you with a horsewhip."

"Get your whip, you old buzzard. Sniper, I'm tellin' you for the last time. Go in and pack a suitcase. You're coming with me. I'll attend to this old tightwad who works his nephew to death—just to save a hired man's wages."

"Gosh, Bunny, I couldn't."

"You can and will."

Simon Parmalee glared at his nephew. "Get in that house and stay there!" he raged. "I'll fix you later."

He wheeled on Bunny.

"And as for you…"

One strong arm shot out. Simon grabbed Bunny by the elbow. But the goalie pulled free. "Keep your hands off me," warned Bunny. "Go on, Sniper. Get moving."

Sniper headed toward the house. Clearly, Uncle Simon's farm would be no place for him after this. His heart was pounding as he bolted through the door of the shabby dwelling.

In the kitchen, he hesitated. He wavered. After all, it was a giant step he was about to take, running away. He had obeyed his uncle for so many years the very thought of disobeying made him shudder. Then he thought of his uncle's endless work assignments, his meanness, and his bitterness. And the razor strap. This was his chance to get away, to play the game he loved—somewhere away from Wheatville. If he stayed, there would be no more hockey for him this season. Uncle Simon would see to that.

He thought of Bunny's words, "I can see you don't have much backbone." Bunny was right. He'd been afraid to be his own person.

Sniper dashed up the stairs to his room, hastily began cramming his meagre belongings into a suitcase.

In the meantime, Uncle Simon, speechless with fury, moved quickly to the stable for his horsewhip. There was something about Sniper's pal that enraged him. He felt the need of a weapon other than his fists.

"Now get out of here, punk!" he shouted, brandishing the whip. "Start moving before I skin you alive."

"I pity the horses if you use that on them," Bunny said. "You're nothing but a bully."

Uncle Simon rushed forward. He drew back his

arm. The heavy whiplash cut through the air. The rawhide slashed across Bunny's midriff.

"Yahoo!" screamed the farmer. Bunny's heavy coat protected him but the fact he'd been attacked made Bunny see red. He jumped in and grabbed Uncle Simon by the arm and tried to wrench the whip from his hand.

Uncle Simon fought back. He punched Bunny in the nose with his free hand and clubbed him over the head with the whip handle. Bunny wrestled the older man to the ground and they thrashed around in the snow.

Sniper came hurrying out of the house, suitcase in hand. He raced down the path and was shocked to see his uncle raise one arm and hit Bunny over the head so brutally that Bunny fell face first in the snow. Growling like a wounded bear, Simon gripped Bunny by the throat and began choking him.

For once, Sniper lost all fear of his uncle. He dropped his bag and plunged in. He threw an elbow to his uncle's head, then slammed into him with a bodycheck that sent him flying into a snowbank.

Bunny sprang to his feet, pushed Sniper aside and muttered, "Stay out of this. I'll finish the job."

Uncle Simon reached for the whip and raised it high, determined to lash out at Bunny again. That's when Bunny hit him with a hard right hand to the jaw. He followed up with a flurry of punches. Thud! Whack! Thump!

Simon squealed and reeled backward across the barnyard. Another punch from Bunny and he bellowed in pain. He fell down, crawled to his knees, put a hand to his bloody nose, then staggered toward the shelter of the barn.

"Wow! You whipped him good," exclaimed Sniper.

"That'll teach him to use a horsewhip on me," Bunny grunted, wiping snow from his clothes. "Now let's get out of here before he decides to use a shotgun on me."

Sniper tossed his suitcase into the back seat of the car and climbed in front.

He heard a howl from the barn. Uncle Simon shrieked, "Don't go with him, Jack! I'll have the law on you. I'm your guardian, remember. I'll call the sheriff."

"Try and stop me," Sniper chirped, enjoying his new found bravado.

The engine roared. The car spun around in the snow and Bunny shouted out the open window.

"So long, you old fart. Get somebody else to do your dirty work."

Sniper sat back and grinned.

"Now I've done it."

"And about time, too," Bunny said with a laugh. "Now we're headed for the big time, Sniper, you and me. We'll show 'em."

But Simon Parmalee wasn't finished with the boys yet. He rushed into the house and called the sheriff's office on Main Street.

"Sheriff Gallagher here."

"Sheriff. It's Simon Parmalee speakin'. My nephew Jack has run off just like Butch did years ago. He's drivin' toward town with some slime-ball goalie who talked him into this. They're in a black Ford—an old one. I want you to watch for them. And when you see them I want you to stop them. I want Jack back."

Sheriff Gallagher smiled. So young Jack Parmalee had finally worked up enough courage to leave old Simon. Good for him.

"I'll watch for them Simon. You know my office window looks right out on Main Street."

"Good. They should be there any minute. You stop those insolent rascals when you see them and call me right back."

"Whatever you say, Simon."

The sheriff pulled his chair closer to the window. "I'll watch for them, all right," he murmured.

Then he reached up and pulled down the blind.

A few minutes later he heard a car race down the street and head on out of town. Sounds like it needs a tune-up, he told himself.

He waited ten minutes and reached for the phone.

"Simon, it's Sheriff Gallagher."

"Well, did you stop them?"

"Sorry, Simon. I didn't see them. Didn't see anything at all. And I was sitting right by the window."

After he put down the phone, he reached over and pulled up the blind. Then he laughed out loud.

Marty stopped reading, put the page down and frowned at Max who waited for his reaction. "Hey, Max," Marty said. "That last scene with the sheriff pulling the blind up and down was funny. And that was some fight back at the farm. I like Bunny. And I like your book so far but I have some questions. And some comments you won't like, I bet."

"Fire away," Max said. "I've got broad shoulders. Remember, I'm just a rookie at this writing business."

"Well, do you really expect readers will believe two teenage nobodies like Sniper and Bunny are going to get jobs in the NHL? With the Leafs? Impossible."

"Maybe you're right, Marty. But remember, the year is 1931. Hockey was a lot different just a few years ago. Fewer scouts. Less money spent on beating the bushes for talent. I hope the reader will be hoping for these two fellows to succeed."

"Well, do they make it?"

Max grinned. "You're going to have to read the

rest of the story to find out."

"O.K. Don't tell me then. Another thing. I think Sniper should have a girl friend, someone to support him besides Bunny."

"Well, how about Brenda?"

"Oh, I forgot about her. That would be good. But you better have him write her some letters or phone her. She'll lose interest if he doesn't."

"Hmm. That's worth considering."

"One more thing, Max. You don't use enough big words. If you throw in some big words—like flatulence for farting, for example—or eccentric to describe Uncle Simon, the reader will think you're really smart."

"I'm not trying to prove I'm smart. I'm trying to tell a story. Besides, Dad says I should use the words I'm familiar with. And he says to write about the things I know best. That's why it's a hockey book."

"O.K. then. It was just a suggestion. I hope all authors aren't as touchy as you are. I'm going to read some more. I can't wait to find out what happens when they get to Maple Leaf Gardens."

Marty was about to begin reading again when he had a sudden thought. "Do me a favour, will you, Max?"

"What is it?"

"Put my name in your book. Why not invent a character named Marty Mitchell. He could be a doctor or a lawyer or a hockey star. Will you do it?"

"Sure. I'll insert something in the next chapter. I'll invent a character named Marty Mitchell. You'll be proud to have him bear your name. I'll have it done by tomorrow. You can start reading the script again then."

"Thanks, Max. You're a great brother. I can't wait to read about myself."

CHAPTER 10

HEADING EAST

The journey east had its hardships. Bunny's car was old and the roads were poor. Neither player had much money. Bunny had budgeted for the trip—but only for one traveler. Sniper felt badly that he couldn't offer to pay for gas or food or lodging. One night they slept on a bench in a railroad station. Another they stayed at a YMCA.

Sniper, free at last of Uncle Simon and the farm life he'd come to hate, felt as if he'd been released from prison. And he was in good company. Bunny had youth and ambition and was always in high spirits. He sang and told jokes and whistled as he drove which took the edge off the discomforts of the trip.

"I had a dog once," Bunny said, chuckling at the memory. "This dog loved to come to my hockey games and watch me play. And if my team lost the game the dog would lie down on the dressing room floor and cry his eyes out."

"That's amazing," Sniper responded. "What did

he do when your team won?"

"Gee, I dunno," Bunny said, straight-faced. "I only had the dog for a couple of years."

He burst out laughing and Sniper punched him on the arm. "And I thought you were telling a true story," he said.

Something caught his attention out the window.

They were driving in a heavy rain when they noticed a man walking along the side of the road, his thumb upraised. "There's a poor guy hitchhiking up ahead," Bunny said. "Maybe we should pick him up. It's raining hard and he's soaking wet."

Bunny pulled over and the hitchhiker yanked open the door to the back seat and hopped in. "Thanks for picking me up," he said. He slouched back in the seat and wrung his hands nervously.

"You're welcome," said Bunny, looking the stranger over in the rear view mirror. "Where you headed?"

The stranger said, "There's a town about twenty miles ahead. My folks live there. They'll be surprised to see me. I haven't been home in a long time."

The young man kept fidgeting. He took several glances out the back window. Suddenly, the sound of sirens could be heard from somewhere in the distance. Bunny could see flashing lights in his mirror.

"Cops are coming," he said. "They're after somebody. I'll pull over. Let them pass."

But when he pulled to the side of the road and stopped, three police cars, sirens wailing, pulled alongside, brakes squealing. Doors flew open and uniformed officers, guns drawn, approached the car from several angles.

"Come out with your hands in the air," a deep voice commanded.

Bunny and Sniper exchanged startled glances and then scrambled out of the car, hands above their heads. The hitchhiker dove for the floor.

"You there in back! Out of the car!"

The hitchhiker slowly opened the door and stepped out. He was rushed by two officers who pushed him roughly up against the car and hand-cuffed him.

"That's him!" shouted one of the officers to the rest of the group. "We've got him."

Bunny and Sniper spent the next few minutes answering questions. Eventually, they were allowed to go on their way.

"Don't be picking up any more hitchhikers," a veteran policeman cautioned them. "That fellow you picked up was a notorious killer. He just escaped from prison."

"Wow!" said Sniper. "And we felt sorry for him. What's his name?"

"Why, that was Marty Mitchell. Number one on the ten most wanted list."

"Marty Mitchell?" Bunny exclaimed. "Everybody's heard of that creep."

Sniper shuddered. "Guess we're lucky to be alive."

For the next few minutes they chatted about their close contact with the escaped convict. But soon they were back to talking about hockey again—and their future in the game.

"Next season, when we're pro players with the Leafs or one of their farm teams, we won't be sleeping on benches and eating in crummy diners," Bunny predicted. "We'll be travelling first class."

"But if we don't make it, what'll we do?" asked Sniper. "Uncle Simon would never have me back after what I've done."

Bunny waved a finger at him. "Don't even think of going back. That man is mean and crazy. After all you've told me about the way he treated you over the years, you don't want to ever set your foot on that place again."

"That's true. But farming is all I know. I never had a chance to learn a trade. And I never finished school. Hockey is my only chance. If I don't make good, I don't know what I'll do. It's 1931— and there's a Depression. Thousands of people are out of work."

"You'll make good," Bunny assured him. "We both will. And you're free of that old man. He'll never bother you again."

"That's true."

But both young men were wrong.

Simon Parmalee was a bull-headed, hard-nosed man who could not bear ridicule. In town, in a lineup at the post office, he overheard two men ahead of him talking about Sniper.

"The kid had no choice," one said. "Living with that old skinflint on the farm must have been unbearable. He had no life."

"Best thing he ever did," his companion agreed. "We'll miss him on the hockey team, though. He was the best they had."

"I was driving past the Parmalee place the day Sniper left," the first man said. "Saw a pal of Sniper's beat the heck out of Simon. I almost got out of my truck and cheered."

Simon Parmalee seethed. "If that kid thinks he's heard the last of me, he'd better think again," he grumbled. "I'll fix his future." That week he'd been forced to hire a hand to help with the farm—at twenty dollars a week.

That night he wrote a letter to his son Butch Parmalee, defenseman with the Leafs. It was a colourful and embellished account of Sniper's bad behaviour.

He wrote: Butch, you ain't been a good son to me, running off to play hockey like you did. Now Jack has done the same thing. Only before he left he beat me with a horsewhip and left me to die in the snow. I'm lucky to be alive. If you ever run into that ungrateful cur, don't lift a finger to help him get a job in hockey. It's one way you can make up for treating me so badly. He needs to be punished and so does that loathsome goalie he hangs out with. The two of them ganged up on me and beat me so badly I may never fully recover.

Simon Parmalee knew his son's character. Butch wouldn't go out of his way to do a good turn for anyone—not even his father. But a bad turn was something else.

Butch was just as mean-spirited as his father. On the hockey rink, he enjoyed his reputation for handing out punishment. He led the league in penalties and had already ended the careers of two rival players with vicious bodychecks into the boards.

When Bunny and Sniper reached the city of Toronto, they were exhausted and almost broke. They checked in at the local YMCA. Bunny's first move was to sell the car. After considerable hag-gling at a used car lot, he walked away with twenty-five dollars. He gave half the money to Sniper.

"But I can't take it, Bunny. You've paid the shot ever since we left Wheatville."

"I insisted you come, didn't I? We're partners, aren't we? Pay me back out of your first pay check."

"But there's no guarantee I'll even get a pay check."

Sniper was beginning to realize how big a gamble he was taking, fleeing the farm to travel hundreds of miles to a strange city with no assurance that he'd even be given a tryout with a professional team.

"Listen, pal!" said Bunny. "There's only one thing wrong with you, Sniper. And I'm going to tell you to your face what it is. You've got no confidence in yourself. If you think you're gonna be licked, you'll be licked. I say your one of the best centremen I've ever seen. It's just bad luck nobody ever really scouted you. Now you've got to believe it, too."

"But I'm not..."

"Hush!" barked Bunny. "Quit going meek and modest on me. I don't want to hear it."

Sniper bought some writing paper and some stamps. That night he wrote a long letter to Brenda Bates and told her about his adventures including the story of the escaped convict Marty Mitchell.

Early the next morning Sniper and Bunny boldly walked into the sparkling new Maple Leaf Gardens. It was mammoth. The team was getting ready for a practice session prior to a home game that night.

Bunny sought out Mr. Conn Smythe, the manager and breezily introduced himself.

"My name's Baker, Mr. Smythe. I'm a goalie

from out West. One of your scouts saw me play last year. Said he was interested in me except your team has lots of good young goalies. I figure I'm as good or better than any of 'em so here I am, ready to turn pro."

Mr. Smythe looked at his watch. "We're on the ice in a few minutes. Keep talking," he said, "I can see you're not shy. I'll give you another thirty seconds."

"That's all I'll need," Bunny continued. "This is your lucky day, Mr. Smythe." He patted himself on the chest. "This is your chance to get a look at a world class goalie and…" He nodded toward Sniper. "A chance to sign a world class centreman, too. Meet Jack "Sniper" Parmalee. Sniper's too good for the amateurs he's been playing with so I dragged him along. You'll want to keep him for his shot alone."

Sniper marvelled at Bunny's sales pitch. He noticed that Conn Smythe, a short man with iron-gray hair, was beginning to smile.

"My lucky day, is it?" he said. "Then I'd better run to the bank and draw enough money to sign you two hot shots without so much as a tryout. Imagine having the world's best goalie and the world's best centreman landing on my doorstep. A manager can't get much luckier than that."

"If you did sign us blind, you wouldn't be making a mistake," Bunny said cockily. "But we'd be willing to show you we can at least skate."

Conn Smythe burst out laughing.

"You're something, you are," he snorted. "Reminds me of myself when I was your age. They said I was too small to play sports. But I...well, never mind. We'll take a look at the two of you. But it'll be a quick look. Come with me."

Mr. Smythe introduced them to Tim Daly, the team trainer who dug around and found some equipment for them. "Make sure you leave the gear behind when you two bushers get tossed out of here in about twenty minutes," Daly warned them.

Then they met the coach, Dick Irvin, a stern-looking individual who'd been a star forward in his day.

"I'll be blunt. We're not planning any changes to the roster," Irvin told them outside the dressing room door. "And if we were, we'd not likely be adding a pair of rank amateurs. So don't get your hopes up. But Mr. Smythe has a soft heart. He likes those movies where the unknown actor in the wings gets a chance to take over the leading role—the understudy—and becomes a star. He keeps thinkin' it'll happen in hockey. But it never does."

CHAPTER 11

THE TRYOUT

Sniper and Bunny could sense the veiled hostility toward them the moment they entered the Leafs' dressing room. When Bunny shouted a cheery, "Hi yah, fellows," he received only a few grunts in return. A few minutes later, a couple of the regulars came over to introduce themselves and wish them luck.

A swarthy, unshaven player with bulging muscles sidled over. Sniper recognized him immediately even though they hadn't spoken in years.

"Hello, Butch," he said, extending his hand. "Guess you're surprised to see me here."

Butch Parmalee ignored the hand and asked bluntly, "What brings you here, kid?"

"Mr. Smythe is giving us a tryout, Butch. This is my pal Bunny Baker. He's a goalie—a good one."

Butch nodded curtly, then laughed. "You're wasting your time. Neither one of you has a chance. The old man must be daft, letting you on the ice with us." He pushed a finger in Sniper's

84

chest. "Especially you, cousin. This is a man's league, kid, and you were always a wimp." He turned and walked away.

"So that's your cousin," Bunny whispered. "No wonder you never got along with him. He should be on a leash."

Butch wheeled and growled, "What did you say, punk?"

Bunny smiled and said, "Nothin' Butch. I just said what a nice personality you have. And how nice it is you're on the Leafs."

Sniper hid a snicker by bending to tie his laces.

On the ice, Coach Irvin said to Bunny, "You get a break. Our backup goalie called in. He has the flu and can't be here. So tend that goal over there." To Sniper he said, "Go sit on the bench. I'll call you when I want you."

Meanwhile, Butch Parmalee and his defense partner, Red O'Brien, met at the boards.

"Two fresh young punks are tryin' to muscle their way in," Butch said, grinning wickedly. "It's a no-brainer. Let's give 'em the works."

O'Brien, short of brains but a brawny brute, licked his lips. "Anything you say, Butch."

Butch spread the word among his teammates. His cousin and the brash goalie needed to be taught a lesson. If one or both of them got hurt in the process, who's to care?

"Today we scrimmage," the coach said. "McRae,

Provost and Gilmour on one line. Morrison, Larocque and Cherry on the other. He called two defensemen over. "Parmalee and O'Brien. Play in front of Baker, the new kid in goal. Give him plenty of help. He'll need it."

"Sure, boss," Butch Parmalee said, winking at O'Brien.

Play began. It was Sniper's first glimpse of professional players in action. Their speed, precision and accuracy amazed and delighted him. When a pass was made, it was executed sharply. There was none of the stumbling and fumbling that characterized hockey in Wheatville.

"These fellows really know how to play the game," he said to himself.

He watched the tall centre, Kelly McRae, handle the puck effortlessly. No waste motion there. His stick was like a rapier in the hands of a skilled fencer. He would break up a rush with a swift thrust of his stick, flip the puck to an uncovered wing, swoop toward the defense, snap up a return pass and make a hard, accurate shot on goal. With eager, intelligent wings like Provost and Gilmour alongside, taking instant advantage of the openings he made for them, McRae made the game look easy.

Sniper always had to play down to the level of his wings. He had known the frustration of seeing his hard passes bobbled or missed by slow-footed teammates. He had been obliged to try for solo goals when his Wheatville wingers hadn't been able to keep up. Eager but inept, they had struggled to convert Sniper's crisp passes into goals, even with the puck cradled firmly on the blade of their sticks and an open corner of the net just inches away.

"Maybe with a couple of wingers like Provost and Gilmour, I could go places," he told himself.

Bunny Baker, meanwhile, was getting little protection in goal. Morrison, Larocque and Cherry stormed in on him time after time, breezing right through the porous defense of Butch Parmalee and Red O'Brien.

Morrison scooted through on a breakaway with suspicious ease. Bunny gave him a peek at an open corner. When Morrison shot, the opening was gone. Seconds later, Larocque sifted through and drilled a high shot. Bunny banged it aside with his glove. An instant later, he leaped across the net to deflect a shot with his stick.

At rinkside, Conn Smythe nodded his head approvingly. He knew the defense had no interest in helping the newcomer. And he'd seen young Baker make a series of sensational saves off some pretty smart forwards.

That took goal-keeping!

Sniper also saw the lack of effort by his cousin Butch and the big lout O'Brien.

"Give the goalie some help!" he yelped from across the ice.

"Shut your mouth, rookie!" Butch shouted back.

Irvin blew his whistle and waved at Sniper and some third stringers. "Get out there, kid. Let's see what you can do."

Then he switched goalies. "I don't want you facing your pal," he muttered. "I want you facing Joe Ransom, one of the best in the business."

Sniper found himself at centre playing with two wings he'd never met. But he knew the names of the defensemen he faced—Butch Parmalee and big O'Brien. And behind them in goal was Joe Ransom—one of the most highly rated netminders in the league.

Sniper was nervous but once the puck was dropped, his anxiety passed. With the smooth ice beneath his skates, a stick in his gloved hands, this was where he felt he belonged.

The rival centre was determined to win the face-off but Sniper slipped the puck away from him, swung around and then streaked up the ice. He shifted fast toward the defense, saw that his left wing had broken clear and whipped over a pass.

Parmalee and O'Brien ignored the pass receiver. They were intent on smashing Sniper into the ice. Butch caught him in the jaw with an elbow and O'Brien clubbed him over the shoulder with his stick. Down he went. But he scrambled back up, in time to see Ransom kick out a shot from the left winger.

Sniper raced in for the rebound, sidestepped a lunge by O'Brien, darted past Butch and got his stick on the puck. He let go a high drive.

Ransom was the most surprised man in the rink when it came. The shooter had been off balance and Ransom expected the shot to be low and weak. Instead, the puck streaked over the top bar and Ransom ducked frantically.

His cousin Butch had taught Sniper that high shot many years ago, before they had a falling out. It was designed to frighten any goalie. Butch approved of the tactic, although Sniper always wondered if it was taking unfair advantage. There was always the chance he could injure a goalie with it and he didn't want that. Still, it had won games, and he hadn't hurt anyone yet. So it had become part of his style.

Goalie Ransom circled his net. He whacked his stick on the ice and glared at Sniper.

"I've ducked away from a lot of high drives in my time but that was one of the most vicious, bullet-like shots I've ever encountered," he mumbled to himself.

Moments later, Sniper wiggled free of his check, took a pass out from the corner and gunned another shot at Ransom.

Zip!

Again, the shot was high. It sailed over Ransom's head, nearly parting his hair. Ransom cursed.

Then one of Sniper's wings controlled the puck behind the net. He passed it out.

Butch Parmalee charged Sniper. He missed and tumbled to the ice as Sniper stepped aside. Sniper snared the pass and twisted back. He sped across the goal crease and whipped in his backhand shot. Ransom's body jerked upward. He was anticipating a sky-high drive. The puck caught the open corner and dropped to the ice.

Ransom charged out of his net and went eye-to-eye with Sniper.

"Bean me with one of those high ones, kid, and I'll open you up with my stick." Then he turned to glower at Parmalee and O'Brien. "I thought you two were going to take care of that pest. He's making you look like clowns from Barnum and Bailey."

Sniper could barely suppress a grin. "I just scored on the great Joe Ransom," he told himself. "Some big league forwards go a whole season without doing that."

"Those two farm boys have a lot of grit," Conn Smythe said to Tim Daly, the team's trainer. "I like what I see."

The trainer smiled. "The boys aren't giving them much of a break. They're trying to run them right back to the bushes where they came from."

"Think I don't know that," sniffed the crusty manager. "When I played, I never used to give a newcomer a break, either. I'd break a few sticks on him, though."

Sniper and Bunny got a load of work that morning, more than they ever expected. Despite the lack of effort by the defensemen in front of him, Bunny made a dozen sensational saves. Finally McRae skated by his net and grudgingly admitted, "You've got class, kid. Keep up the good work."

CHAPTER 12

A PRACTICAL JOKE

Sniper's hard shot caught the attention of everyone. He was able to drill the puck on goal from impossible angles and even when thugs like Butch and O'Brien were harassing him.

The two mean-spirited defenders decided it was unwise to concentrate on the rookie too thoroughly. It left his wings wide open. Sniper took all the punishment they dished out and gamely came back for more. At the same time, he fed perfect passes to his mates and the result was several goals. Two of them he scored when Ransom braced himself for high drives. The veteran goalie was enraged when Sniper slipped the puck swiftly to a corner of his net—right along the ice.

"You...you...busher!" Ransom exploded.

Coach Irvin skated to the boards. He had a question for Conn Smythe. "How many guys you seen who could slip pucks by Ransom so easily?"

"Darn few."

"Right. Shooters like the kid—Sniper is it?—

don't fall out of the sky. He may have a few rough edges—he doesn't need that blazing high shot, for example—but I think we have ourselves a hockey player."

"Maybe two of 'em."

"Yes, the goalie is good—a natural. But he's not so important. Joe Ransom's past record speaks for itself. He'll be our starter for a long time to come. I like that centre, though. He's fast, he's game and he's got something we need—scoring punch."

When the morning scrimmage was over, Bunny was exuberant. He was delighted with the encouraging words he'd heard from McRae. Sniper, on the other hand, was not optimistic. None of the other Leafs had uttered a kind word to him. He hadn't received so much as a slap on the bum with a stick, a traditional way a hockey man says, "Good job." He was accustomed to getting his bum slapped in Wheatville.

"We showed 'em," Bunny whispered. "You scored on Joe Ransom, didn't you? Three times at least. And they might not have scored even once on me if those bums in front of me hadn't stood there like fence posts."

"Still, it's going to be hard to make this team," Sniper replied. "They stick together. My wings wouldn't feed me a pass to save their souls. My own cousin tried to hammer me into the fence more than once. And that goofball O'Brien..."

"Never mind," Bunny whispered, giving his buddy a light punch on the arm. "We gave them something to think about. Believe me, we're gonna make this team."

Sniper showered and began to dress. But there was something wrong with his clothes. His good shirt was tied in knots. His pants were soaking wet. Somebody had wiped their skate blades on them. And his shoes were full of tap water.

"Oh, no," he groaned.

He looked around. All the other players were grinning, waiting for his reaction. They broke into laughter at his stunned look.

"Wet yer pants, did you?" Butch shouted across the room. "Seems to me you did that when we were on the farm together."

Sniper stood there in his underwear, angry and embarrassed. He started across the room toward Butch. But Bunny leaped up and held him back.

"Don't start anything, Snipe," he cautioned in a low voice. "That's exactly what Butch wants. Throw a punch and they'll all jump you for sure."

Sniper realized the advice was sound. He forced a laugh. "Guess the joke's on me, fellows. Those pants of mine needed a good washing." He picked up one of his water-filled shoes. "I'm real thirsty after scoring all those goals today." He put the heel of the shoe to his mouth and took a swig, pretending to drink. The room exploded in laughter. Then Sniper spit a mouthful of water on the floor. "Yuck! I think I swallowed a minnow," he said, sticking out his tongue. There was more laughter.

McRae was standing nearby and smiled at Sniper. "That was smart, kid. Good thinking. If you'd fought them, they'd have shaved every hair on your head."

Coach Irvin stuck his head in the door and nodded at Sniper and Bunny. "Mr. Smythe wants to see you two in his office."

Bunny's face split into a grin. "We'll be right there," he said.

In the office, manager Smythe stared at them for a moment. "Your pants are all wet," he said to Sniper. "How come?" Before Sniper could answer, he waved a hand and said, "Forget it. I don't want to know. But you better not sit down. Listen to me. I guess you know you have a lot to learn about hockey—a lot to learn."

"Yes, sir," agreed Sniper.

But Bunny cut him off. "Anybody who can beat Joe Ransom three times in ten minutes hasn't much to learn about shooting. And I figure I've learned about all I can about goaltending. So how about it, Mr. Smythe? Do you want us or should we shop ourselves around to some other teams?"

The manager grinned. "You've got some ego, kid. You talk a good game but I must admit you play a good one, too. Tell you what. Stick around for a few days. We'll advance you both some money for expenses. I want to see if you were one-day wonders. Play like you did today and we may talk contract."

"Fine with us," Sniper said. He almost shouted, "Whoopee!"

"Yep, we'll do it," Bunny added calmly. "But remember, the better we perform, the more you'll have to pay us."

The manager's eyes twinkled. He laughed at Bunny's arrogance.

"I guess you know our backup goalie is laid up. You'd better be ready to take his place for tomorrow night's game. And Sniper, we'll find you a proper uniform. Maybe the coach will throw you in for a minute or two."

Grinning like a pair of lottery winners, Sniper and Bunny left the arena and went out to celebrate. They each had twenty dollars expense money in their pockets.

"There's an ice cream parlour down the street," Sniper said. "Let's treat ourselves to a banana split."

Sniper's shoes squeaked and squished as he walked along and water dripped from his pant legs. People they passed stopped to stare at the kid who left a trail of liquid along the sidewalk. And when the people looked back, they noticed the young fellow next to him had something plastered in white chalk on the back of his jacket: I'M A GOOFY GOALIE.

On their way home, Sniper and Bunny passed a store with a sign FRESH FISH FOR SALE.

"Let's go out back," Sniper suggested.

Behind the store was a garbage can.

"What a stench!" Bunny said, turning away. "There are rotten fish in there."

"Right," Sniper said, chuckling. He pulled a small towel from his pocket and a paper bag. "And we're going to take a couple."

"We're not eating rotten fish," Bunny declared.

"They're not for eating," said Sniper. "They're for a friend of ours."

That night, Sniper wrote Brenda Bates another long letter, telling her all about their surprising tryout with the Leafs. He hoped she'd send an answer.

Marty turned the page and put it down. He started laughing. "That was so great," he chortled, waving the manuscript in the air. "It was so funny." He laughed some more. "Wait until the kids at school see this."

"What are you talking about?" Max asked.

"Me! I'm in your book. And you made me out to be an escaped convict, a murderer facing life in prison. That's hilarious. It's the best part of your book so far."

Max grinned. "I thought you might be mad at me. I thought of naming you as one of the players. Or a referee."

"No, no, no. The guys on the hockey team will crack up when I tell them my name is in your book—as an escaped convict. They'll howl. It's perfect, Max. Thank you."

Marty read on for a few minutes. He turned to Max who was at the typewriter. "So the Leafs really gave Sniper and Bunny a tryout. That was interesting."

"Glad you think so," was Max's response.

"I have another question, Max. How come you're using real hockey names in your book?"

"You mean like the team name Leafs? And Conn Smythe?"

"Yeah. Wasn't Smythe the famous guy who bought the Leafs and built Maple Leaf Gardens?"

"That's right. And because the Leafs are my favourite team I thought I'd use that name in the book. I even wrote Mr. Smythe and asked his permission to use his name."

"And he wrote you back?" Marty said, surprised.

"He did. He even sent me a Leaf calendar. Told me to use any of the Leaf names I wanted, no matter what era they played in. He said he'd like a copy of the book if it ever gets published."

Marty was impressed. "Well, don't get all

swollen-headed but I think it's a pretty good story. So far, anyway. Guess I'll read some more. I want to know why they're collecting rotten fish. And if you'll find a way for Marty Mitchell to escape from prison again."

Max grinned. "I doubt it. But you'll find out. Well, guess I'll keep on writing. I'm getting close to the end."

CHAPTER 13
SOMETHING FISHY ABOUT BUTCH

Sniper and Bunny arrived at the arena early the following evening. The dressing room was deserted, except for the trainer, who soon left to sharpen some skates.

"We're early. Let's go to the snack bar for coffee," Bunny suggested.

"You go," Sniper urged. "I've got something I want to do. I'll join you there in a few minutes." He held up a paper bag and wrinkled his nose.

"Gotcha," said Bunny.

Alone in the room, Sniper walked to Butch Parmalee's stall and opened the paper bag. Holding his breath and working quickly, he inserted small bits of chopped fish into the deep pockets of Butch's hockey pants, pockets that kept his pads in place. Sniper went to the wash-room, disposed of the bag, washed up and left. He went to the snack bar where he joined Bunny for a coffee. They read the sports pages of the local paper for half an hour. Then they returned to the dressing room.

Butch Parmalee snorted like a nervous horse when he looked up from his stall and saw his cousin Jack slide unobtrusively into the Leafs' room.

"I can't believe it," he roared in disgust. "Don't tell me you're going to play tonight!"

"No, I'm just going to be warming the bench," Sniper replied. "And Bunny is going to be backup to Ransom."

"Speaking of Ransom, you'll be warming a slab in the morgue if you try to bean him with any more of those wild shots," Butch threatened.

"They were hardly wild. And you taught me how to shoot them high."

"Well, keep 'em down from now on."

Ransom, sitting nearby, overheard the conversation. "Hey, if they weren't wild then you were trying to bean me," he said, his face red.

"Guess he was trying to put you out of the game so his pal would grab a goaltending job," suggested Butch.

This hadn't occurred to Ransom—until now. He stopped putting on his gear and leaped up. "If that's what you were doing..."

"But I wasn't," Sniper protested. "I just did it to get you to duck. To make you worry about the next one..."

"You made him duck, all right," Butch laughed,

stirring up the goalie's lingering anger. Butch began hauling on his pants. He stopped and sniffed. "Boy, my equipment stinks," he muttered.

"It sure does," said O'Brien, shifting down the bench. "I'm not sittin' next to you tonight." Other players fanned the air with their hands and shifted away from Butch.

Ransom continued to growl at Sniper. "Takes more than bushers like you to make me duck."

Sniper didn't reply. He wanted to be on good terms with the Leafs. If they would only let him.

Other Leafs began to complain of Butch's body odour.

"You really stink, Butch."

"Don't you ever shower?"

"Don't come near me, skunkhead."

Butch was totally confused. He examined every piece of his equipment, sniffing furiously. He examined the bottom of his shoes, looking for dog poop. He could not tell where the awful odour was coming from.

A few minutes later the Leafs skated onto the ice to face the Red Wings. Sniper's jaw dropped when he heard the great buzz of the crowd, saw the ceaseless flow of moving people in the stands which were banked high from the rail seats to the girders. And there among the girders, high above the ice, was Foster Hewitt's famous gondola. Hewitt's play-by-play radio broadcasts were becoming famous from coast-to-coast. At the far end of the ice, sliding back and forth in goal, was the great Detroit netminder "Sugar" Jim McHenry, the league's shutout king. It was difficult for Sniper to believe that he, a rank amateur who'd been playing in Wheatville's shabby old rink a few nights earlier, was on the same ice with him, and with many of the other top professionals in the game. And just a day after his unexpected tryout.

No wonder his cousin Butch had been astounded. No wonder some of the other Leafs, many of whom had spent years toiling in the minors, resented his presence. And Bunny's, too.

Sniper wasn't aware that Coach Irvin had been tinkering with his third forward line, unable to find a decent centre to fill the bill. Tonight he planned to give Sniper a few minutes' trial—in a real game—to see how he stacked up against Bubba Rolph, who'd been holding down the position .

In the pre-game warmup, the Leafs took their customary shots against Joe Ransom, getting him ready.

When it came Sniper's turn, Ransom challenged him. "Come on, busher. Make me duck!"

Sniper took the puck and dashed in. From thirty feet out he blasted a shot low to the corner. But the puck hit a tiny chunk of hard ice and deflected up. Ransom threw up a gloved hand to protect his face—an instant too late. The puck, driven with the force of a bullet, zipped over his glove and hit him smack between the eyes. Ransom pitched to the ice where he lay, motionless.

There was a quick roar of apprehension from the crowd.

Coach Irvin and the trainer rushed out, Irvin's eyes ablaze with anger.

"See what you've done!" he yelled at Sniper. "Those high shots of yours are killers."

Butch Parmalee skated by and scowled at the horrified Sniper. "That's one way of making sure your buddy gets to play," he sneered. He leaned against the sideboards and repeated his accusation to some fans. He was surprised when they backed away, holding their noses. "Geez, what a stench!" one of them said, gagging.

Ransom was carried back to the dressing room. He was still unconscious. Sniper remained in shock. It had been a perfectly normal shot. But the chunk of ice...

But that did little to alter the perception that he'd deliberately injured his team's starting goalie. Already a distorted version of the incident was spreading throughout the arena.

In the press box, a veteran reporter stated emphatically that the rookie had drilled another of his high shots and Ransom gamely had refused to duck. He said it was a callous act by Sniper, putting Ransom out of business for the benefit of his buddy, Bunny Baker. He would repeat his opinions during the first intermission when he was interviewed on the radio broadcast.

By then Ransom had regained consciousness and the trainer had removed his equipment. The club doctor thought Ransom would be all right, aside from a couple of black eyes and a slight concussion. But he ordered him to a nearby hospital for further observation.

"Give him a week, maybe two," the doctor said. "Then he should be good as new."

"Sure, if he isn't puck shy," said the coach. "I've seen goalies who never come back after taking a shot to the head like that." He turned to Bunny. "You'll have to go in, kid. That buddy of yours certainly gave you a break."

Conn Smythe took his coach aside. "I saw Sniper shoot," he said. "The shot wasn't high. It hit something and deflected up. I don't believe Sniper would deliberately put his own goalie out of commission. It's just one of those things."

But if Conn Smythe ruled Sniper blameless, the same couldn't be said of his teammates.

Butch Parmalee was delighted to spread the word that Sniper's high shot had done the damage, a shot fired with the express purpose of sending Ransom to the hospital. His teammates appeared to accept Butch's assessment without question.

From the drop of the puck, the Red Wings

launched a smashing attack. They were a talented team, fast and flashy with real scoring punch. And they hoped to take advantage of the break that thrust an untried rookie into the Leafs' goal.

Rene "Rocket" Renaud, their top scorer, streaked in, faked a shot, pulled Bunny out of position and slipped the puck to his left winger who was hot on his heels. The winger whipped the puck toward the opening but it wasn't there any more.

Bunny made the save, then quickly dropped to his knees for another quick stop when Butch fumbled the rebound and lost it to Renaud.

The visitors sent out their second line. Their coach had instructed them to pressure the goalie, to make him falter. If he blew up the Red Wings could treat themselves to a scoring spree.

But Bunny Baker didn't blow up. When Butch Parmalee drew a foolish penalty and the Leafs were short-handed for two minutes, the Red Wings rattled shot after shot at the rookie. He dodged, darted, deflected, making saves from every angle.

It was McRae who stunned the visitors with a breakaway goal—shorthanded. He stole the puck from Renaud, raced down the ice and slammed the puck into the Red Wings net.

Butch returned from the box and Irvin sent out his third line. Sniper didn't get the nod. Bubba

Rolph grinned at him as he jumped the boards and skated in for the faceoff.

During the first intermission, there was a new attitude toward Bunny. It couldn't be called friendly but it was at least respectful. The Leafs appreciated his play and realized he'd filled in for Ransom in spectacular fashion.

The Red Wings kept the heat on in the second period, launching a series of brilliant attacks that had the Leafs reeling.

Butch drew a second penalty, five minutes this time, and once again Bunny held the fort. He knocked down a high shot for the corner, fell on it and smothered the puck as Red Wing forwards poked at his pads, trying to knock the puck loose.

From the corner faceoff, the puck clicked from stick to stick as the Red Wings moved the puck around inside the Leafs' zone. There was a sudden shot but Bunny did the splits and kept the puck out. He caught the next shot in his glove and nailed a third with the blade of his stick. He went down under a sprawling heap of bodies as the Red Wings tried to shove him into the net, puck and all. There was a jubilant howl from the crowd as Bunny was found, face down, hugging the puck underneath him. Most of the hometown fans stood and applauded and Bunny acknowledged their handclapping by waving his goal stick.

Bunny's puckstopping gave the Leafs a lift.

McRae finished off a neat passing play by scoring his second goal and moments later Morrison connected, beating "Sugar" Jim McHenry with a low corner shot from close in.

It looked like the Leafs, thanks largely to Bunny, were in the driver's seat, heading for a win. In the third period, McRae completed his hat trick with a shot through McHenry's legs.

Coach Irvin decided it was time to give Sniper a little ice time. "Get on out there in place of Rolph," he said.

Sniper felt as empty as a drum as he slid off the bench and moved in for the faceoff outside the Red Wings' blue line. He had Hawkes on his left wing and Barron on his right. Opposing him at centre was Abel, the Red Wings' captain.

Stage fright gripped Sniper, froze him for a moment when he realized that thousands of fans were watching his every move. Then, when the puck fell and he and Abel smacked sticks, the fear was gone and a feeling of excitement and determination took over. He trapped the puck and sent a hard pass over to Barron, who seemed unprepared to handle it. To the fans, it looked like the pass may have been badly timed, a bit inaccurate.

Sniper raced over for the loose puck and skimmed a long pass to his left-winger Hawkes. Hawkes raced away with it and inside the Red Wings' zone, sent a return pass to Sniper. But

Sniper had to pull up short and reach back for the pass, almost falling as he did so.

Abel stole the puck and darted away from Sniper before he could regain his balance. Abel was fast but Sniper was faster. He overhauled him, wrestled the puck away, and wheeled back. He cut in on the defense, pulled one defenseman toward him, and passed to Barron, who had stepped in ahead of the play, was offside.

Suddenly, Sniper realized what was happening. The clannish Leafs weren't going to co-operate with a player who had deliberately injured their star goalie. The Leafs held a big lead, the game was winding down and Hawkes and Barron weren't interested in exerting themselves, especially if it made Sniper look good.

Manager Conn Smythe had seen Sniper's passes. He knew they'd been right on target. He tapped Irvin on the shoulder. "Hawkes and Barron are trying to make Sniper look like a stumblebum," he said.

"Yep. But what can I do? They'll just tell me they're accustomed to Rolph and know his style. They'll say this new guy can't pass a potato with a snow shovel. Look! They're at it again."

On the ice, Sniper broke free of Abel's check and was in the clear. But Barron, instead of passing him the puck, threw it over to Hawkes. Sniper had to scramble back to get on-side but the fraction of delay spoiled Hawkes' chance. He scowled at Sniper and the crowd howled in exasperation. The play, to most of the fans, made Sniper look like a beginner.

Seconds later, Renaud and Abel moved in on Bunny with Sniper backchecking hard, hounding Abel. Butch stumbled and fell down, leaving an opening. Abel's hard shot bounced off Bunny's broad chest. He fell to his knees, the puck at his feet. Abel swiped at it. Renaud took a whack and Sniper was there, too, trying to clear. Sniper pushed the bouncing puck toward the end boards, but he was horrified to see it slide off his stick, glance off the goal post and plop into Bunny's net. The red light flashed. Goal for the Red Wings!

There was a stunned silence. Then a rumble of disappointment from the crowd. Bunny Baker scrambled to his feet, his eyes wide in surprise.

Sniper heard Abel chuckle, "Nice goal, kid."

Bunny looked at Sniper, then covered up his feelings and managed a grin. He'd been hoping for a shutout and thought he'd had one. Now it was gone.

"Accidents happen, Sniper," he said, aware that his buddy felt worse than he did.

Head down, Sniper turned and skated to the bench. Irvin greeted him with sarcasm. "That was nice," he remarked. "A lovely goal. Too bad it was at the wrong end of the rink."

Sniper heard Butch chuckling. "That's my dopey cousin—Dummy Parmalee. Just ruined his pal's shutout."

Sniper was devastated. He could still see Bunny's look of consternation when the puck rattled off the post and fell inside the net.

He tried to analyze the play. He'd been harried, of course, and had to clear the puck fast. But where were his wings? If they'd covered their checks, if they'd come in to help out, the accidental goal might never have happened.

But the fact remained it had happened. He had to accept it. To the fans it must have looked like a bonehead play by a clumsy, boneheaded player. He had to accept that, too.

The game ended at last.

CHAPTER 14

BUNNY SPEAKS OUT

Back in the dressing room, eyes on the floor, Sniper unlaced his skates. His stint with the Leafs was over. He was certain of that. Perhaps his friendship with Bunny was over, too. He couldn't hope to be forgiven.

And then he felt Bunny wedging in next to him on the bench. The goalie's hand slapped his knee.

"Hey, forget about it, pal," Bunny said. "It was just one of those things."

"I'm so sorry, Bunny. I was just trying to clear the puck. Abel was there, about to tap it in. I had to work fast because Renaud was there, too. And then..."

"Don't you think I saw all that?" demanded Bunny. "You made the only play you could. It was just bad luck that it bounced in off the post. Forget about it."

"But it cost you a shutout. And in your first pro game."

Bunny smiled and said confidently, "I'll get

myself plenty of shutouts before I grow a white beard and move on to oldtimer's hockey. The crowd seems to think I did pretty well."

"You were great out there. I'm so proud of you."

Bunny looked around the room. "It makes me mad that the guys haven't got any sympathy for you. I bet every one of them has kicked the puck into his own net once or twice. Well, I'm gonna do something about that."

And without another word, Bunny leaped up on the bench and shouted, "Hey!" In a voice loud enough to be heard in the arena lobby.

There was silence. Surprised faces turned toward him.

"This is no speech," Bunny began. "I just want you fellows to know that I had a few people sympathizin' with me tonight because I missed a shutout. Well, that doesn't bother me as long as the team won the game. Now the guy you should be feelin' sorry for is Sniper. He had the bad luck to score that goal on me and he feels terrible about it—a blamed sight worse than I do. Maybe if he'd been out there with a couple of wingers who weren't tryin' to sabotage his chances..."

"Now hold on, Baker," snapped the coach. "None of that..."

"Coach, when I'm under contract to this team, I'll take orders from you. But I'm not under contract just yet so I'll have my say. And I say I'm not too impressed with a few fellows on this club. So whether I play with you this winter or not doesn't really matter."

Sniper was appalled at Bunny's words and continued to stare at the floor.

"Sniper is the sort of player this club needs," Bunny continued. "He didn't lay out Ransom on purpose and if I thought he did I wouldn't have anything to do with him. And if his wings had given him some support tonight the puck wouldn't have gone in my net and he wouldn't be feelin' so bad."

There were shouts of protest from Hawkes and Barron but Bunny kept on talking. "You know you let Sniper down. Have the guts to admit it."

He turned and stared at Butch, who had just stepped out of his hockey pants and was scratching his bum.

"There's another guy in this room who's tried to make Sniper's life miserable and he should be ashamed of himself because he's Sniper's cousin, for cryin' out loud."

With that, Butch Parmalee leaped across the room, his face as red as a goal post.

"Why, you screwball," he roared. "For ten cents, I'll knock you into next week."

"And I'll do it to you for nothing," Bunny said hotly.

He jumped off the bench and punched Butch

squarely in the nose. Butch howled and swung back. He slapped Bunny hard on the side of his head. Bunny countered with a hard shot to the stomach and Butch went "Oooph!" He wrestled Bunny to the floor. Players leaped in and dragged them apart, huffing and puffing but still eager to fight.

"Come outside with me and I'll tear you apart," Butch threatened. Someone threw him a towel and he wiped blood from his nose.

"I'll come outside," Bunny snarled. "But we'll settle this in the alley 'cause I don't want to be seen outside with you."

Still enraged, Butch kicked out and sent a pair of hockey pants flying in the air. From inside the pants, several pieces of rotten fish flew out and players ducked.

"They're my pants," he exploded, pointing an accusing finger at Bunny. "And it was you who put the fish in 'em. My wimpy cousin wouldn't have the nerve to do it."

Bunny grinned. "Not me, pal," he taunted. "Guess again. Besides, why would anyone try to make you smell worse than you already do?"

Some of the Leafs burst out laughing.

"Good point," murmured McRae.

Manager Conn Smythe had been watching the incident from the doorway. He shouted two words, "That's enough!" He moved to the centre of the room and waved a finger under Butch's red nose. "Sit down and cool off!" he demanded. He whirled on Bunny. "You calm down too. I want to see you in my office in five minutes. And bring Sniper with you."

Conn Smythe sat behind his desk and regarded the two young men who stood in front of him—Sniper, lean and young and handsome; Bunny, short, round of face, almost always smiling. But frowning now, wondering if he'd just blown his chance with the Leafs.

"Before I begin, I want you to know, Baker, that you did a good job in goal tonight."

Bunny's smile came back. "Thanks, Mr. Smythe."

"Until Ransom gets back, we've got to have a goaltender. So if you'd like to come along, we leave on a road trip tomorrow. We'll sign you to a contract and when Ransom comes back, chances are you'll be our backup. Either that, or you can go to the minors."

"I'd rather play in the minors, Mr. Smythe. Backup goalies don't get much work."

"Maybe you won't have to go to the minors. If Ransom comes back puck shy, it may mean there's a place for you."

"I'd hate for it to happen that way," Bunny said earnestly. "He was hurt by accident and I sure hope he's not all washed up."

"I hope so, too, Bunny. And by the way," he said, turning to Sniper, "I know Ransom's injury was an accident. I saw your shot. I know you weren't aiming high. Listen, kid, you have lots of ability. You have all the skills. You didn't get a chance to show them tonight. How old are you, anyway?"

Sniper was tempted to lie, to tell Mr. Smythe he was going on twenty. Instead he said, "Seventeen."

Conn Smythe sighed and opened a drawer. He pulled out a paper.

"I understand your uncle is your guardian. Well, it didn't take long for him to find out that you were with us. Maybe Butch had something to do with that. Anyway, your uncle says in this telegram:

> *My nephew Jack not of legal age. I am warning you. Do not sign him to a contract without my consent. Legal action will follow if you do.*

Bunny exploded. "Why, that interfering old busybody!"

Sniper was shocked. The possibility of legal action to thwart his hockey ambitions had never occurred to him.

"Can he do this to me?" Sniper asked.

"I'm afraid so, son," Conn Smythe replied. "He's your legal guardian until you're eighteen. When's your next birthday?"

"Not until May of next year. So I can't play hockey for you until then."

"Not unless you petition the courts to have your guardianship set aside. You'd have to build a case. That'd take time and money. A lot of money. Lawyers never come cheap.

"Tell you what, son. I'd be willing to put you on our reserve list. Sign this form and I'll give you a dollar to seal it. That gives the Leafs first rights to your services when you are able to play."

Sniper thought about it for all of two seconds. Then he signed and took the dollar.

When the two buddies left the office minutes later, one was under contract to play, the other was without a job.

"I'm happy for you, Bunny," Sniper said. "Congratulations."

"What are you going to do now, Sniper?"

"Don't know. Find some kind of a job, I guess. We'll see."

"You can live with me until you find something. I've got a regular paycheck now."

"Maybe I'll stay for a day or two. But let you support me? No thanks, pal."

Sniper managed a grin and held up a bill.

"What's so funny?" said Bunny.

"I'll bet I'm the only pro hockey player in history who ever signed a contract for one dollar."

Bunny chuckled. "Well, you can frame it or you can spend it."

"Let's spend it," Sniper said.

CHAPTER 15

SNIPER DISAPPEARS

Bunny left the next day for a two-game road trip. In those two games, Bunny really established himself. The hard-hitting Black Hawks scored two goals against him, both scored when the Leafs were playing short-handed. Bunny stopped 43 shots in a 3-2 win. Two nights later, against the Habs, he stopped 40 shots in a brilliant shutout over the league's highest scoring team.

Conn Smythe and Irvin agreed that the rookie was a "natural", more impressive in his road appearances than he'd been in his first game on home ice. The other Leafs, with the exception of Butch and O'Brien, began to warm up to him.

Bunny came back to town bearing newspaper accounts of his outstanding play. One reporter predicted that Joe Ransom, recovered from the injury that had given Bunny his big chance, would soon be relegated to the minors.

Ransom looked up Butch Parmalee and Red O'Brien the moment the team returned. He was even more positive in his belief that Sniper had deliberately injured him. He nursed a burning hatred for Sniper and the goalie who'd supplanted him in the net.

"Looks like you two guys gave the new goalie plenty of protection in the last two games," he said accusatively.

"No, we didn't," Butch snapped back. "But he doesn't need any protection."

"We don't like him any more than you do," O'Brien added. "But we're not going to throw away our jobs just to get even with him. Smythe and Irvin are already suspicious of us."

"Looks like I'm the big loser here," Ransom said bitterly.

"Sniper's a big loser, too," Butch said. "He's been paid back."

"How?"

"My old man is his guardian, see. So I wired Pa and told him Sniper was here. Pa sent Smythe a telegram tellin' him the kid wasn't of legal age, that he'd send the law after Smythe if he signed him."

"That's something," sniffed Ransom. "But it don't get me my job back."

"You haven't lost it yet," O'Brien told him.

"No, but judging by the way this Baker's playing, I'm gonna have trouble keeping it."

The others felt the same way. But they didn't say so.

When Bunny checked in from the road trip, he went directly to the small apartment he'd rented. There was a note on the kitchen table.

Dear Bunny:

You've been fighting my battles for me long enough and I appreciate it. But now it's time I learned to stand on my own two feet. If I hang around here I'll only be a drag on you. I can't tell you where I'm going because I don't know. But you'll be hearing from me. I'll send you the money I owe you as soon as I can.
Your pal,
Sniper

P.S. I got two great letters from Brenda Bates while you were gone. She's the nicest girl I ever met.

"Well, I'll be darned," Bunny muttered. "Why did he have to go and do that? But I'll say this. I have to admire the kid's independence. He's never had much of a chance to stand on his own two feet. More power to him."

Bunny left for the arena where he ran into Joe Ransom getting in his gear for the morning workout.

"Hi, Joe," Bunny greeted him cheerfully. "How you feeling?"

"Feeling good enough to take my job back," Ransom snapped curtly.

Butch Parmalee was standing nearby, struggling into a set of shoulder pads.

"It's great to have you back, Joe," he said. He nodded at Bunny. "The kid goalie had a couple of lucky games on the road. I call it beginner's luck. But his ticket to the minors is on the way. You'll see."

McRae looked up. "Don't be so sure, Butch," he said softly.

"Gee, Butch," Bunny said flippantly. "You're such a diplomat. I guess I shouldn't have unpacked my bag."

They took the ice and Coach Irvin divided his team for a scrimmage. Bunny was in goal for one squad, Ransom for the other. McRae snared the puck from the faceoff and broke in on Ransom. Deliberately, he shot high and hard at Ransom. The goalie saw the black rubber driving toward him and involuntarily ducked away from it. He recovered, made a last second stab at the puck and missed. The puck ripped into the net.

It hadn't been a difficult shot, not the kind that would give pro goaltenders much trouble. There was only one reason Ransom had muffed it.

He was puck shy!

As the scrimmage continued, this fact became painfully evident. He shied away from half a dozen more high shots. He simply couldn't help it, even though he made desperate efforts to cover up his weakness.

When the workout was over, he approached Irvin. "I felt good out there, coach. Do I get to start in our next game?"

Irvin shook his head slowly. "I think you're still a little rusty, Joe. Let's wait a few more days before we put you back in."

Ransom knew what that meant. Irvin had lost confidence in him. He twisted his mouth bitterly. In the dressing room, he snarled at Bunny.

"You tell that buddy of yours to stay out of my way from now on. If I see him again, I'll kill him."

When Sniper disappeared from the small apartment he'd been sharing with Bunny, he was prompted by something more than his Uncle Simon's cruel blow. He realized he had been letting Bunny fight most of his battles for him. It was Bunny who'd urged him to leave the farm; Bunny who'd talked the Leafs into giving him a tryout; Bunny who'd fought with Butch on his behalf.

"That's over," he murmured to himself. "I'm almost a man. It's time I started acting like one."

He hitchhiked to a small city a hundred miles away. He sought work but jobs were scarce and his skills were limited.

He moved on, sleeping on benches in railroad stations. He shovelled snow off driveways for enough money to buy a meal. He helped a man unload a truck full of lumber. He worked as an usher in a movie house, filling in for a worker who went to California to attend a funeral. When the man came back, Sniper moved on.

He was hitchhiking to a place called Ironwood when a police car pulled up. "Where you going, boy?"

"Ironwood, sir."

"Don't you know that hitching rides is dangerous?"

"Yes, sir. I do know that." Sniper thought of the time he and Bunny had picked up the notorious killer Marty Mitchell. "But I don't have much choice. I try to be careful. I don't have enough money for bus fare."

The officer felt sorry for Sniper. A hard rain had soaked him through.

"Get in the car, son. I'll take you into Ironwood."

Sniper slept in a jail cell that night. In the morning, the officer gave him fifty cents.

"That'll get you breakfast."

"Thank you, officer."

"But I'm going to give you a ticket."

Sniper's heart leaped. He was about to be charged. He had no money to pay a fine.

"A ticket?" he gulped. "For what?"

The policeman laughed.

"For the hockey game tonight. I can't go. I'm on duty."

"Hockey game?"

"Yep. Semi-pro hockey. Ironwood's playing Pine Grove for first place in the Industrial League. You ever see a hockey game?"

Sniper admitted he'd seen a few. He took the ticket and heard the officer shout, "No more hitch-hiking," as he left the police station.

The calibre of hockey in the Industrial League did not impress Sniper. It was the lowest rung of hockey's ladder. He watched the Ironwood Aces first line centre, an overweight man named Adams. He was slow and awkward and lacked a shot. But he loved to fight and opponents jumped aside when he lumbered up the ice. Sniper knew that he could play better than Adams. Much better.

After the game, he found his way down to the Aces' dressing room. He sought out the manager, Stollery, and thought of how his pal Bunny would handle the situation.

"How about a tryout, Mr. Stollery?" he asked brashly. "I can see you need a good centreman. That tortoise you've got there now is on his last legs."

The manager glared at him. "And who are you to be calling my centre a tortoise?"

"I'm a hockey player. Give me a tryout and I'll show you."

"Who did you play for?"

"Wheatville. A team out West."

"Never heard of it. Go away. Don't bother me."

Even Bunny would have admired the way

Sniper faced Stollery.

"I played for a team a lot better than that—the Leafs."

"The Leafs, eh?" Stollery said, at first showing respect. Then he became suspicious. "Why ain't you still with 'em? You look too young to be a big leaguer."

Sniper told him the story.

"Come around in the morning," said Stollery. "We'll see what you can do."

Sniper was there, bright and early. He'd slept on one of the arena benches, after getting permission from a sympathetic night watchman. In his bag were his skates. During all his trials, he'd never parted with them.

There was coffee and some doughnuts in a box in the dressing room. Sniper was told to help himself. He didn't have to be asked twice. Stollery handed him an old uniform and a stick and sent him out.

It took a few minutes before Sniper found his skating legs. But when he did, in a scrimmage, he broke fast down the middle, pulled the defense apart, swooped in on goal and whipped a backhand shot to the upper corner of the net. The goal left "Tiny" Thomas, the goalie, shaking his head.

"Oh, my," said Stollery. "Pretty!"

Half an hour later, the Aces knew they had a new centre in their midst.

I'm glad he's goin' to be playin' for us and not against us," Thomas grunted as the players left the ice. "He scored three times on me and I haven't figured out how he did it yet."

Stollery met with Sniper outside the room. "I can get you a job in the factory. It pays thirty bucks a week. And we'll give you an extra twenty-five to play for the Aces."

Sniper grinned. "Suits me. When's my first game?"

"We play the Beavers on Thursday night. But here's the thing. I don't want any crabby uncles coming around making trouble. Or your cousin Butch reading about you scoring goals for us in the sports pages. He could cause a lot of trouble, too."

"That's true," Sniper agreed.

"So why don't we give you a new name? We'll put you down on the roster as Jack Lee, O.K.?"

"I suppose. But changing names bothers me a little..."

"Hey, movie actors do it all the time. They're entertainers, just like hockey players."

"Well, when you put it like that..."

So Sniper Parmalee, also known as Jack Lee, signed to play hockey for the Ironwood Aces.

He wrote a letter to Brenda Bates and told her all about his new situation—and his new name. And he listed the Aces' arena as a return address.

CHAPTER 16

WITH THE ACES

Ten minutes into his first game—against the Beavers—Sniper looked down to take a poorly-aimed pass.

Wham! A big defenseman smashed him squarely across the face with gloved hands and a tightly held stick. Sniper went down in a heap while the crowd yelled. He crawled to his feet, dazed. There was a salty taste in his mouth. It was the crudest, hardest check he'd ever received. It was a cross-check—violent and illegal.

He wondered why the referee hadn't blown his whistle. If ever there had been a play that called for a penalty...

The play raged around the Aces' net. Finally "Sockeye" Doran trapped the puck in his glove and held on. The whistle blew.

Stollery called Sniper to the bench.

"You hurt?"

Sniper shook his head, tried to grin. "I'll be O.K."

"Listen, kid," said Stollery. "You were playing too well to suit them. That defenseman was told to slap you down."

"Well, he slapped me down all right. But the referee..."

"Sniper, if you start squawking about the referees in this league, the fans will ride you out of town. Hockey is a tough game here. Maybe after somebody almost gets killed, they'll clean it up. Your only option is to go back at that defenseman and make him respect you."

Sniper nodded grimly. He was playing for a living in a bush league now. So were the others. Only the toughest survived. They were playing to protect their jobs and their paychecks.

"Next shift, out you go," Stollery told him. "This time make 'em like it."

Sniper made them like it. He grabbed the puck and flashed in on the Beavers' defense. Harrison, the burly rearguard who'd smashed into him, swung at him wildly with stick and body but was left in Sniper's wake, swinging like a rusty gate in a wind storm. Sniper swooped in, held his shot, then flashed across the crease and backhanded the puck into the upper corner of the net.

Sniper had served notice that it would take more than a dirty crosscheck to slow him down.

Moments later, Sniper dashed into the corner of the rink, chasing a bouncing puck. Harrison slipped in behind him, lunging with his stick. He hooked it under Sniper's right skate and pulled. Sniper went down, sprawled, and skidded into the boards hard, arms up to protect his head. The fans yelled with fury as the whistle stopped play.

Sniper groaned and crawled to his feet. Harrison was grinning contemptuously. The referee waved Harrison to the penalty box but he waited, waited to see how the flashy rookie would respond.

Sniper threw his gloves to the ice, skated up to Harrison in two quick strides. "If you're looking for trouble, pal, look at this!"

And he swung. Harrison tried to duck but he wasn't quick enough. Sniper's left caught him flush on the jaw. He stumbled back, off balance. Sniper hit him again, this time with a right. It staggered the defenseman who tried to fight back. But another punch staggered him even more. His skates went at odd angles and then went out from under him. Down he went, holding his hands to his bloody face.

The fans were howling with joy. Several Aces moved in and pulled Sniper back. Four or five Beavers hauled Harrison to his feet, held him back as he half-heartedly tried to get at Sniper. The referee chased them both to the penalty box.

It was one of the few penalties Sniper had ever drawn in his career. But he didn't regret it. Had the referee been on the job in the first place, it wouldn't have happened.

His counter attack on Harrison made Sniper an even bigger favourite with the Ironwood fans. Not only that, he served notice on the league that he would not be intimidated.

When he skated out of the box and moved into the Beavers' zone, he was checked hard but fairly. Against fair checking he could always hold his own.

Sniper was discovering that if you don't want to be trampled in life, you've got to assert yourself. Not necessarily with a fistfight which, unfortunately, was a tradition in hockey. It was odd, too, how little it took to make people respect you. "Perhaps I shouldn't have bowed to Uncle Simon's will so easily," he told himself. "Oh, well, what's done is done."

He wondered if fighting might someday be gone from hockey. He wouldn't miss it. And he worried that young kids might feel they had to fight in order to succeed.

The Aces won their game that night by a 7-2 score and Sniper was the number one star with three goals and two assists.

That same night in the big league, the Leafs were coasting to a win over the Red Wings, and Bunny Baker, the sensational rookie netminder, was heading toward another shutout, his fifth of the season. With a 4-0 lead in the third period, the whitewashing seemed assured. But the two defensemen in front of Bunny, Butch Parmalee and Red O'Brien, weren't about to make it easy for the rookie.

Butch might easily have cleared a loose puck from the crease if he'd been more alert and reached for it faster. But a Red Wing forward got there first and slapped the puck into Bunny's net.

Two minutes later, Bunny made a brilliant save and steered the rebound to Red O'Brien, standing off to the side. O'Brien muffed it, then passed it without looking, right onto an opponent's stick. Bang! Another puck landed in the Toronto net.

"Wake up, you bums!" Bunny shouted at Butch and Red.

"So you lose your shutout," Butch snarled back. "Big deal!"

After the game Bunny walked up to the manager, his face grim.

"That's it. I'm through, boss."

"What?" gulped Mr. Smythe.

"I said I'm through. Either Parmalee and O'Brien leave this team or I'll leave it. Whenever we have a comfortable lead, when the odd goal against me won't cost us a win, those two clowns let up. They don't give me any protection. I've had it with them."

Conn Smythe was aware of the problem. Now Bunny had brought it to a head. And Bunny could afford to talk to him like this. His first few weeks in the league had been sensational. Still, Smythe had to save face.

"I'm running this team, Bunny. And I'll decide who stays and leaves."

But two days later, he traded Parmalee and O'Brien to the Rangers for a veteran defenseman and a promising left-winger.

CHAPTER 17

SNIPER SPARKLES, RANSOM SAGS

Early in March the Aces were holding first place in the Industrial League by a wide margin. Sportswriters gave most of the credit to Jack Lee, the rookie centre, who had provided the team with a scoring punch it had previously lacked.

Scouts from half a dozen teams looked him over and made proposals but Sniper turned them down. "Maybe next season," he told them. Sniper and Stollery knew that Uncle Simon could—and would—have him barred from playing hockey—for at least another few weeks. What's more, Sniper was hoping he'd have a place in the Leafs' future, re-united with his pal Bunny.

The first week in March, the Aces lost their star goaltender. "Sockeye" Doran, the team's promising youngster, broke his hand and would be gone for several weeks. Stollery made arrangements for a replacement but he neglected to mention the newcomer's name.

Two nights later, when Sniper entered the team

dressing room prior to a game with the Beavers, he was stunned to see his old nemesis, Joe Ransom, sitting in a stall.

Ransom was surprised, too. He had looked over the Aces' roster. The name Jack Lee meant nothing to him.

Ransom was surly and bitter. He'd gone down the hockey ladder fast since the night Sniper's high shot had knocked him out. He'd come back puck shy, a condition he'd been unable to conquer and it had ended his big league career.

Out of work for weeks, he'd convinced Conn Smythe that he'd been cured—by a hypnotist—and was ready to make a spectacular comeback. Smythe wasn't convinced and told Ransom to join the Ironwood club.

Stollery's hand fell on Sniper's shoulder. "Want you to meet our new goalie, Jack," he said. "And Joe, this is our top centre, Jack Lee."

Ransom's lip curled when Jack stuck out his hand and said, "Hi, Joe."

Ransom struck Joe's hand away. "I won't shake with a guy who's runnin' around using a fake name. The same guy who ruined my career."

The other players in the room gasped. Stollery's eyes bulged with astonishment.

"Sorry, Joe," Sniper said softly, "You've got me all wrong. Maybe someday you'll realize it." He turned and walked away.

The Aces couldn't understand it. None of them knew Sniper's real name. But they knew something had happened in his past to make Ransom despise him. Whatever it was, it was difficult for any of them to think badly of Jack Lee. He had long since been accepted as a good teammate and sportsman.

The players dressed and went out to warm up. Ransom had just arrived so there had been no chance for him to work out with the team. Stollery wasn't concerned. Ransom had a reputation as a big leaguer, didn't he? He'd conquered his problems and would soon be on his way back up.

In the warmup, Ransom made his stops with the poise and smoothness of a world-class netminder. Some of the Aces wondered why the Leafs had ever let him go.

But Sniper knew why.

The game got underway.

Sniper scored a goal in the opening minute. He laid down a perfect pass to his left winger outside the Beavers' blue line, took a return pass inside the line and one-timed a shot that slammed into the net.

But the Beavers fought back and took three hard shots at Ransom. They were all low and Ransom steered them aside expertly. The Ironwood fans shouted encouragement. This new goalie was hot!

Moments later, he turned back half a dozen more shots when the Aces were playing short-handed. Ransom had the rink in an uproar.

His play seemed to give the Aces a lift and midway through the period, Sniper set up a linemate for a pretty goal and on the same shift scored one himself. Aces 3, Beavers 0.

But in the second frame, the Beavers stormed back. A defenseman took a hard shot from the point. It sailed high, whistling toward Ransom's head. He ducked and pulled away, then made a last second grab at it. He missed. The puck hit the net below the cross bar.

The goal upset Ransom and the Beavers knew it. They began to pepper him with high shots, from long and short range.

He let in another, a high drive that might have sailed over the net if he hadn't jumped nervously and pulled back. He got a glove on it but he was jittery now, unsteady. The puck skipped out of his mitt and into the net.

The Beavers tied the score in the third. Aware of Ransom's weakness, they continued to shoot high from any angle. One of their wingers managed a breakaway and blasted the puck from twelve feet out. It rose sharply and Ransom flinched, turned his head. The puck ripped into the upper corner. Tie score.

"One more goal, Sniper," Stollery pleaded. "You

can do it."

He got it by slamming a pass over to his streaking winger. Raced up the middle and pushed through the defense. Was there when the return pass came and cut in sharply. He faked a shot from outside the crease. The goalie leaped to block it but the shot never came. Sniper deked around him and slipped the puck neatly into the corner of his cage. The hometown crowd screamed its approval.

The Aces won 4-3.

"Good thing we've got a goal scorer," Stollery declared, mopping his brow. He turned and half whispered to the trainer. "But what are we gonna do for a goaltender? It's a cinch this guy Ransom is all washed up."

Back in the hotel room that the Aces had arranged for him, Ransom decided he was through with hockey. The Beavers had spotted his weakness in a matter of minutes. It wouldn't be long before every club in the league knew he was a sucker for a high, hard shot. Try as he might, Ransom had been unable to resist shying away from those drives, hadn't been able to conquer his weakness.

Sniper had pulled the game out of the fire in the last minute and earned a standing ovation. Ransom hated him for it and blamed his downfall on the young phenom.

Ransom found some writing paper and dashed off a letter to Butch, care of the Rangers.

You'll be interested to know that your hotshot cousin is playing here in Ironwood under an assumed name—Jack Lee. I plan to get even with him for what he did to me if it's the last thing I do. Maybe you should tell your old man he's here. He might want to do something to stall Sniper's hockey career.

In the morning, Ransom went out to mail the letter. He dropped it in a box on the street corner, turned, and ran into Stollery who was stepping out of a cab.

"Just the man I'm looking for," Stollery said. "I've got news for you, Joe. I want to tell you we've decided to give you another chance."

"Another chance?" Ransom was surprised. "I figured you were going to get rid of me."

"To be honest, I was. I didn't know I'd hired a goalie who couldn't face a high, hard shot. But young Jack Lee stood up for you. He says you're a goalie, I say you're not. But he persuaded me to give you a second chance."

When Stollery drove away. Ransom strolled back to his hotel, deep in thought. He was puzzled. Why would Sniper Parmalee speak up for him? He couldn't figure it out.

In the hotel lobby, Sniper was waiting for him. Ransom glared at the teenager. "I didn't know I was so popular," he growled. "Seems like everybody in the organization is coming to see me."

Sniper ignored the jibe and the venomous look.

"I got off work this morning so I could see you, Joe," said Sniper.

"Why bother? We've got nothing to say to each other."

"Now listen here, Joe. I told you you've got me wrong. You think I deliberately laid you out so Bunny could steal your job. That's bull. It was an accident. I shot low and the puck hit some bad ice and went high. I know I have a reputation for shooting high—Butch taught me that when I was a kid—to keep a goalie on edge. But I didn't shoot high on you. Honest.

Ransom could tell from the look on Sniper's face that he was speaking from the heart, that he was sincere. Sniper plunged on.

"Joe, you're the first goalie I ever hit in the head. You've got to admit the shot would have been wide if you hadn't stepped into it. I can usually place those shots where I want them. I could fire half a dozen shots at your head and never touch you."

"Yeah. Well, I'm not about to let you try."

"Face it, Joe. You've gone puck shy. If I'm to blame for it—even though it was an accident—I want to make up for it. Come on down to the rink with me and let me give you a little workout." Sniper held up a mysterious parcel he'd been carrying under his arm. "I've got something here I think may help a lot."

Ransom hesitated. Perhaps he would go. What Stollery had told him about Sniper speaking up for him had begun to alter his opinion. Sniper seemed genuinely interested in making amends. And that package he held up—what was that all about?

"Let's go," he said gruffly. "But you hit me in the head again and I'll lay you out."

At the rink they donned their hockey gear and skated out onto the ice. Sniper looked at his watch. They had an hour before any of the other players would arrive. He unwrapped the package he carried and produced a baseball catcher's mask.

"Wear that on your head, Joe. If I do hit you with a shot, it won't hurt. But I'm going to drive some high ones at you. Maybe after awhile, you'll get the idea that you're not going to be hit. You won't pull away from them."

Dubiously, Ransom donned the heavy mask and took his place in net.

Sniper stood about twenty feet in front, a number of pucks at his feet. He began whipping shots high, within a foot or two of Ransom's masked face. Instinctively, the goalie pulled away from the shots.

"I'll shoot the next ones slower," Sniper said. He directed his shots high but with much less steam. Two or three skimmed past Ransom's head, but this time, preparing to feel them strike the mask, he held firm.

For the next half hour he fired shot after shot at Ransom. Some struck the mask and bounced harmlessly away. After awhile the veteran goalie found himself facing the shots with something of his old-time disdain.

When Sniper tired, Ransom took off the mask. "This is a great idea," he said. "Why don't all goalies wear these things?"

"Don't know," Sniper said. "Maybe they're afraid they'll be called gutless if they do. A few years ago, a young woman wore a fencing mask in college hockey. Makes sense to me, but then, I'm not a goalie."

Ransom slipped the mask back on. "A baseball mask may not be ideal for hockey," he said. "It's a little hard to see the puck at my feet. But if it cures my problem, I'm all for it. Take a few more shots, Sniper."

On the way back to the dressing room, Ransom began to whistle. "Sniper isn't such a bad guy after all," he murmured. "I feel badly I mailed that letter to his cousin."

At that moment, in the Leafs' front office, a hockey scout was talking excitedly to manager Conn Smythe.

"So I'm coming through Buffalo, boss, when a newspaper guy I respect told me I should check out a kid playing in the boondocks, in a dump called Ironwood of all places. The kid's name is Lee—Jack Lee.

"So I hop over there and watch a game and guess who's playin' in goal for the Ironwood Aces? Joe Ransom, that's who, tryin' for a comeback."

"Poor Joe," said Conn Smythe. "He'll be lucky to stay in that bush league. He's gone puck shy."

"Joe was pathetic," the scout agreed. "But his team wins in spite of him. This kid Lee scored a bunch of goals including the winner with a minute to play. He's a natural; a checker, a goal scorer and what a shooter!"

"Lee, huh? Well, maybe we can sign him up for next year. Too bad we can't get him for this year, Winky, if he's as good as you say he is. What with the Cup playoffs around the corner and us needing some help at centre..."

"Boss, you *have* got him for this year!" The scout laughed. "I'm savin' the best for last. The kid's name isn't really Lee. It's Parmalee. Sniper Parmalee! He made a commitment to you and the Leafs months ago. For a dollar bill. Remember?"

"Sniper? Of course I remember." Mr. Smythe

rose from his chair and began pacing the room. "The young man has a lot of talent," he said. "A lot of talent. He disappeared for awhile. And now you say he's playing in some industrial league under the name Lee? But listen, Winky, you know we can't use him until he's eighteen, don't you? His uncle—his guardian—is an old crab who won't let him play."

The scout shrugged. "Boss, if you bring the kid back to the Leafs, his uncle isn't going to know the name Jack Lee. How long will it take before he finds out we're using Jack Parmalee? He'll wake up in Wheatville or whatever hick town he lives in sometime next summer. What can he do then? Playoffs will be over and the kid will be eighteen— out of the old crab's clutches."

A grin spread across Conn Smythe's face. "Winky, how many concussions did you suffer in all those years you played for the Leafs?"

"About a dozen."

"Well, I'm glad to see they didn't affect your brain. That's a great idea you just gave me."

CHAPTER 18

BACK TO THE LEAFS

Joe Ransom improved rapidly. It wasn't long before the puck shy goalie regained his lost confidence and most of his old-time form.

With Ransom stopping 'em and Sniper banging in goals, the Aces lengthened their lead in the Industrial League race. They went on to capture the league title with ease and went unbeaten in the playoffs, to capture the Ironwood Cup.

Ransom's success meant more to Sniper than his own. He was proud to have started a player on the comeback trail, proud to have converted an enemy into a friend.

And Ransom was grateful.

"I'm ashamed of myself for wanting to get even with you, Sniper," he said. "If it hadn't been for you I'd be on the hockey scrap heap."

In the meantime, their old team, the Leafs, having won the league championship, was involved in the long Stanley Cup playoff grind. They ousted the Bruins in a semi-final series, four games to three.

The Leafs had emerged from the regular season with a formidable injury list. Kelly McRae had a bad knee and a sore shoulder. Both starting defensemen were taped from toe to scalp. There wasn't a regular who hadn't suffered some form of bruise or hurt.

Conn Smythe knew he'd need some reinforcements. Two days before the Cup playoffs began—a best four-out-of-seven series with the Rangers—he called Bunny Baker into his office.

"I want to talk to you about a pal of yours," he began. "Sniper Parmalee—the kid we couldn't use because his uncle threatened us?"

Bunny's guard was up. "What about him?"

"Have you heard from him lately?"

"Well, yes. I had a couple of letters. He's been playing hockey in some backwoods league. His team, the Aces, won the championship and he was leading scorer. He's counting on you bringing him to training camp next year. He'll be of age then."

Conn Smythe grunted. "You can rest assured we'll do that, Bunny. Listen, you're not telling me anything I didn't know. I know what name he's playing under, too, and all the rest of it. I even know he just signed up for night school. He wants to get more education."

Conn Smythe laughed at Bunny's look of surprise. "I've had reports on him. I've talked to my chief scout, Winky Davidson. With our crippled lineup

147

we may need that boy."

"Uh, oh. His uncle will put a stop to that."

"No he won't. Not if he doesn't know about it. Here's what I want you to do, Bunny. Go down to Ironwood and see Sniper. We want to get him into at least one game of the playoffs. After we use him, his uncle can argue his head off if he wants to. Get it?"

Bunny whistled. "I get it. But why don't you call him yourself and invite him back?"

"Because Stollery, his manager, doesn't think he'll report. He says Sniper wants to forget about hockey until next season. Apparently, he's planning to go west and see some girl he's fallen for. And maybe have a confrontation with his uncle. Then he's going to come back and start night school."

Bunny frowned. "So you want me to go down there and persuade him to come back. Why not send Winky Davidson?"

"Because Sniper doesn't know Winky. You're his pal. You can persuade him to come. Winky Davidson sometimes says the wrong thing at the wrong time."

"Okay, I'll do it."

"That's the idea, Bunny. But remember, not a word to anyone. This is our secret. Don't even tell Sniper we want him to play. Just tell him we want him to come to Toronto to see some playoff hockey.

Let him know we haven't forgotten him.

"Get some expense money from accounting, hop on the train and be on your way. I know the kid will come back if you go to see him personally. But when you get back, let me break the news about him playing for the Cup."

"Sure, Mr. Smythe, I'll bring him back," Bunny promised.

When Bunny reached Ironwood later that day there was a joyous reunion. The two rink buddies hadn't seen each other in weeks and there was much catching up to do.

"Fine guy you turned out to be," Bunny said in jest. "Skipped out on me. Just left with only a note."

"I had to learn to stand on my own two feet, Bunny. I don't let people push me around anymore. Anyhow, I wrote you after I got settled here."

"Sure you did. And sent me some money. You didn't owe me anything."

"Sure I did. I sponged off you all the way across the country."

"It was nothing," said Bunny. "Hey, I hear you've been a sensation in this bush league."

"How about yourself?" Sniper replied. "Getting into the Cup finals in your first season in pro. But what brings you here? The series gets underway the day after tomorrow."

Bunny nodded. A grin split his face. "Yeah. But

Conn Smythe sent me here to ask if you'd consider being a guest of the Leafs for the series. A rinkside seat and all expenses paid."

Sniper was surprised. "You're kidding!"

"Nope. It's the truth. Conn Smythe wants you for next season. I guess maybe he wants to butter you up before he starts talking contract."

Sniper shrugged. "I figured Mr. Smythe had forgotten all about me. Remember, I told him I'd sign a real contract once I'm free of Uncle Simon's guardianship. Let me think about it overnight. I was planning to go out west for a few days. Then I'm going to start some classes..."

"Yeah, I heard. At night school, right? Well, that can wait and Brenda can wait, too."

Sniper took a deep breath. "I don't know, Bunny. Let me think about it."

Bunny was exasperated. "You don't have time to think about it, Sniper. Mr. Smythe's gotta know. We've gotta be on that train tomorrow."

The goaltender was bursting to tell his friend that he'd be playing in, not watching, at least one of the final games for the Cup. But he'd promised to let Mr. Smythe give Sniper the good news. And Bunny could keep a secret.

But his secret did not stay a secret for long.

"I'll let you know in the morning," Sniper promised. "I'll have to ask for a leave of absence from my job."

The next morning, Sniper met Stollery who quickly arranged for a leave of absence. "The Leafs should be bringing you back as a player, not a spectator," was Stollery's only comment.

On the way out of Stollery's office, Sniper ran into Joe Ransom and told him the news. To his surprise, Ransom seemed to know more about the situation than he did.

"Yes, I heard the Leafs were sending for you."

"You did, Joe? It's supposed to be a secret. They're not going to play me, of course, but at least they're inviting me back as a guest of the team."

Ransom smiled knowingly. "You don't have to be cagey with me, Sniper. I know you want to keep things hush-hush so the Rangers won't call your uncle and sic him on you and keep you off the ice."

"No, Joe, you've got it wrong. The Leafs aren't asking me to play."

It was Ransom's turn to be puzzled. He fished a letter from his pocket. "Well, explain this to me then."

Sniper read the letter. It was from Sniper's cousin Butch.

Dear Joe:

It was mighty good of you to tell me how my goofy cousin Jack wound up in Ironwood. It didn't bother me at all that he was playing in that bush

151

league so long as he stayed there. But the other day one of the Leafs' scouts, a fellow named Winky Davidson, got talking to a fellow who was a pal of our manager with the Rangers. This Winky guy said the Leafs were going to pull a surprise against us in the playoffs and bring in a kid named Jack Lee. The name wouldn't have meant anything to me if you hadn't tipped me off that Lee was really Jack Parmalee. I'll make sure that everyone knows Lee—or Parmalee—ain't eligible to play until he's eighteen, which is some time off. I told you we would get even with Mr. Smarty Pants.

Keep your head up—especially on those high shots, ha, ha.

Your pal,

Butch

Sniper was astounded. Obviously the Leafs had planned to use him in the playoffs, giving him a chance to realize the dream of every hockey player— to play in a Stanley Cup match. A feeling of bitter disappointment swept over him. Once again, his mean-spirited uncle and his cousin stood in his way.

Joe Ransom saw the look on his face.

"I'm real sorry, Sniper. I'm sorry I wrote Butch about you being here. But that was when I was mad at you and when I blamed you for getting me kicked off the Leafs. Now, I've gone and blown your chance of getting into the playoffs. I can see how upset you are."

Sniper tried to smile. "That's all right, Joe. It helps that you showed me this letter from Butch." He shrugged. "I can deal with it."

"It's odd that Bunny didn't tell you about the Leafs' plans."

Sniper shrugged. "Maybe he didn't know Conn Smythe was planning to give me a chance. Maybe Mr. Smythe was worried that word would leak out and Butch would find out. And you know what would happen then." He let out a sigh. "I think I'll just forget about hockey until next year. The game is full of disappointments. I'm going to meet Bunny at his hotel. I'll tell him I've changed my mind about going to Toronto. I'll just say I'd rather go out west for a few days."

When Sniper told Bunny that he wouldn't be making the trip after all, his friend was stunned.

"But you've got to come back with me, Sniper. Conn Smythe needs you. That's why he sent me. We've got to leave today."

"You didn't tell me the Leafs planned to use me in the Cup finals. You know they can't do that."

Bunny sighed. "I was keeping that as a surprise. Mr. Smythe told me to let him give you the good news. Besides, he didn't want the press to get wind of his plans. Kelly McRae is in bad shape. If he goes down, the Leafs will need you at centre— at least for one game. He's got you on his playoff roster as Jack Lee. Nobody is supposed to know about this."

"Well, Butch Parmalee knows. And you can bet Uncle Simon will soon know."

"Aw. That kills it," Bunny said, throwing up his arms. "He'll sue the team."

"Yes. He and Butch will see to it that I can't play. Maybe I should put hockey aside until next season."

"Now listen, Sniper," Bunny said. "Don't go back to being Mr. Meek on me. My orders are to bring you back. How do you know Conn Smythe hasn't hired a bunch of lawyers to go over your situation, to jump in if Butch and your uncle try anything? Maybe your uncle got kicked in the head by a pretty smart cow and is in a coma for all we know. But I can't go back without you."

Bunny could see that his friend was still undecided. So he added the clincher.

"Are you going to stand by and let a miserable old man and that cow flop he calls a son keep you out of the Stanley Cup finals? I'll be bitterly disappointed in you if you do."

Sniper's words struck home. When Sniper thought of being robbed of his big chance by a skinflint uncle for whom he'd slaved without pay ever since he was a youngster, and an uncouth lout of a cousin, he seethed with anger. He had learned to stand on his own feet in the past few

154

months. He had matured and gained confidence. He was proud that he was quite capable of looking after himself.

He grabbed Bunny by the arm. "All right, pal. I'll go. If those two skunks related to me think they can push me around, I'll show 'em they won't do it without a fight."

Bunny gazed at his friend. "That's the way to talk," he declared. "Let's go!"

CHAPTER 19
DITCHING A GUARDIAN

On the train to Toronto, Sniper and Bunny discussed ways and means of blocking any possible action on Uncle Simon's part; but every idea they came up with had flaws.

"The fact is he's still your guardian and you're under his control for another couple of months, until you're eighteen," Bunny said. "You may just have to wait him out."

Leaf manager Conn Smythe was happy to see Sniper again.

"I hear you've been making quite a hockey player of yourself," he said. "And you've grown a bit and put on some weight. You needed a few more pounds. Has Bunny told you what I have in mind?"

"Yes, but somebody has already upset the apple cart," Bunny said morosely.

"How come?"

Mr. Smythe bristled when he was told how Butch Parmalee had found out about the plan to use Sniper in a playoff game. "That Winky and his big mouth," he snorted. "Well, I don't know what to do next."

"I do," said Sniper. "I just need the use of a telephone. I need to start fighting more of my own battles."

On home ice, playing before a howling mob of hockey enthusiasts, the Leafs jumped into a series lead in the Cup finals against the Rangers with a 2-0 victory. Reporters and broadcasters were lavish in their praise of rookie goaltender Bunny Baker. One reporter wrote: "Young Baker made a dozen spectacular saves. He's embarking on a Hall of Fame career."

In the second game, Kelly McRae decided the outcome in the double overtime, poking in a goal that gave the Leafs a 3-2 win.

Sniper stayed in Toronto when the series moved to New York for the next two games. He worked out on the arena ice with some junior players and listened to the games on the radio. He felt badly for Bunny when his friend was beaten in overtime twice—both on deflected shots. The teams returned with the series knotted.

Meanwhile, he had made several calls to government agencies and even one to a lawyer back in Wheatville. He told Bunny he was still waiting for return calls.

"It's the weekend," Bunny told him.

"Government people are slower than molasses. And lawyers! They'll get back to you if they think you're a big shot—with money."

"I'm not a big shot," sighed Sniper.

The fifth game proved costly for the Leafs. Sniper saw Kelly McRae, playing hurt, take a vicious check from Butch Parmalee. It was a crosscheck across the back that sent McRae hurtling into the boards. He had to be helped from the ice by his teammates as Butch skated to the penalty box. Butch nudged the penalty timekeeper sitting next to him. "Guess that ends his season," he smirked.

Later in the period, during a goalmouth scramble, Butch drove the butt end of his stick into Bunny's ribs. There was a long delay while Bunny tried to catch his breath.

With McRae out and Bunny injured, the Rangers skated to a 3-1 win. Bunny was beaten on the final goal when his clearing pass was intercepted and the puck was slammed back at him, trickling through his pads.

"Too bad about McRae," Butch told reporters without showing an ounce of remorse. "I hit him cleanly but he musta slipped. We'll win the series in game six. Especially since the Leafs' rookie goalie is beginnin' to crack under the pressure."

"Bunny says you drove him in the ribs with your stick," a reporter told Butch.

Butch just laughed. "What a liar! I never touched the guy."

When Bunny read in the papers that Butch had called him a liar and that he'd predicted a Ranger victory, he was inspired. Despite his bruised ribs, he came up with a brilliant performance back in New York and skated off with a 3-0 shutout. After the game, he stuck his tongue out at Butch Parmalee.

By then, the Leafs had a familiar face seated at the end of their bench. Concerned about Bunny's ribs, Conn Smythe had looked around for an emergency backup goalie.

Sniper heard him discussing the situation with the coach.

Boldly, Sniper asked, "Why not bring Joe Ransom back?"

"Old Joe. He's washed up," Smythe said.

"No, he's not," Sniper replied. "He played great hockey for Ironwood, after he conquered that problem of his. He'll be back in the NHL next season, I'll bet. Playing somewhere."

Smythe gave Sniper an icy stare. "Hmmm," he said.

The following day Joe Ransom joined the team.

The series was tied. The seventh game would be played on Toronto ice. By then, Sniper had resigned himself to being a spectator.

But on the afternoon of the deciding game, Sniper, the media and the fans got quite a shock. Conn Smythe announced to the press that Sniper Parmalee would replace Kelly McRae at centre ice in the deciding game.

A number of reporters descended on Smythe. "Who is this guy," they demanded. "Where'd he come from?"

Conn Smythe explained that Parmalee was Leafs' property. "Signed him last fall," he told them. "He's been playing in the Industrial League under the name Jack Lee."

Immediately, there was a howl of protest from the Rangers. "The Leafs can't use Parmalee," claimed the Rangers' manager. "He's underage. His guardian won't allow it. He'll sue."

To this, Conn Smythe said bluntly, "Sniper Parmalee will play. Let the old man sue."

When the Leafs skated out that night, Sniper Parmalee, wearing number nine, skated out with them. He was a little nervous as he circled the ice.

The crowd buzzed with excitement. Did the Leafs plan to defy the whole league? The Rangers' declaration of protest had been delivered and appeared to be airtight. Yet there was Sniper in uniform, taking warmup shots on Bunny.

Butch Parmalee couldn't believe it. He skated up to the referee. "What's the big idea?" he roared. "My cousin can't play. My old man absolutely forbids it. He notified the Leafs and the league governors. He'll sue the entire league."

The referee shrugged. "Where you been, Butch? In Siberia? The issue was settled hours ago. The league president gave his approval and what he says goes."

Sniper had been watching this exchange and skated over.

"You can't do this, punk," Butch snarled at him. "You're breaking the law."

"As if you never broke it," Sniper snapped. "I remember what a juvenile delinquent you were back home. Anyway, the league heard today from the lawyer I hired in Wheatville. He did some checking for me and guess what, Butch? Uncle Simon never took out guardianship papers for me! He's been my unofficial guardian but never my official guardian. Guess he was too cheap to pay the fee required. So I'm free to make my own choices. You don't like it, Butch, then shove it."

"I'll shove you—all over the ice," Butch threatened. He raised his stick and waved it at Sniper.

The crowd roared, anticipating an altercation. And settled back down when Sniper laughed at Butch and skated away.

The Rangers were rattled by the eleventh hour surprise. Ordinarily, the injection of a new man into the opposing team's lineup means little. But the uproar over Sniper showing up convinced them that he must be special, distinctly above the average substitute.

Thousands of excited fans in the arena, and thousands more listening to the famous commentator Foster Hewitt on their radios, waited eagerly for the opening faceoff.

"You're starting, kid," coach Irvin said, tapping Sniper on the shoulder.

Opposing him was Bill Skene, the blond flash of the Rangers, a second year pro. Flanking Skene were Vance and Hallett, at right and left wing—a pair of tough veterans. Butch Parmalee and Red O'Brien glared at Sniper from their defense positions. Poker-faced Buddy Bradley was in goal.

Most fans thought that Irvin had lost his senses, sending out an untried rookie to start the game. It bordered on insanity.

But Irvin defended the move. He spoke to reporters during the warmup. "Parmalee's no minor league player. He's in perfect condition and he's got a scoring punch, and a shot you won't believe. Sure it's a gamble. But if we lose, well...that's hockey."

Sniper's throat was dry as he moved in for the faceoff. Once the puck was dropped, his jitters disappeared. He focused on holding Skene in check and moving the puck into the Rangers' zone.

But Skene wasn't playing in the Cup final by accident. He was fast and crafty. And he could break like lightning. He was the best opposing centre Sniper had ever faced.

Sniper stuck to him, but Skene faked one way, darted another, picked up the puck and went in for a scoring chance. Bunny made a big save and Sniper tied up Skene's stick before he could whip in the rebound.

"That was close," Sniper murmured as the teams changed lines.

On his next shift, Sniper picked up the puck at his own blueline, broke away from Skene, and streaked away with it. Butch and Red O'Brien were waiting for him. Sniper faked a pass, then cut through between them. He'd have made it if O'Brien hadn't reached out and hooked his jersey, pulling him off-stride. That's when Butch smashed into him. All Butch's accumulated rage and resentment was in that body check. Sniper hit the ice with a sickening jolt. Gasping for breath, he rolled over and almost passed out.

His head was swimming. His lungs were burning. But he saw Skene with the puck, breaking away. Sniper crawled to his feet and gave chase. There was no hope of catching the fleet centre. Skene bolted into the Leafs' zone, his left winger in the clear. A swift pass and the winger went around the defense. He took a hard shot from the side. Bunny made the stop with his chest, but the rebound came out in front. And there was Skene, trapping it for just an instant, then whacking it into the corner of Bunny's net.

Ranger fans at Maple Leaf Gardens—and there were many—cheered with joy. In a Cup final, every goal looms as big as Mount Everest.

Sniper went to the Leafs' bench, winded and sore. And quite discouraged.

He was overwhelmed with a feeling that he wasn't good enough. He lacked the experience to cope with the veterans on the Rangers' roster—especially Skene. He slumped down on the bench and tried to ignore the pain from his aching ribs.

He had been given the biggest chance a rookie ever had—to make his mark in the biggest series of the year—and he was muffing it.

In back of him he heard a remark not meant for his ears.

"The Rangers made a lot of fuss over nothing when they tried to stop the Leafs from using that dud at centre."

Sniper's face was crimson. After all the uproar about his eligibility, it would be a joke if he failed to make good.

Just then, a howl went up and the play was stopped. A Leaf forward was sprawled on the ice, clutching his knee. Butch Parmalee, who beefed loudly to the referee before banging the penalty box door behind him, had slashed him.

"Get out there, Sniper," Irvin barked.

CHAPTER 20
A DRAMATIC FINISH

Sniper scrambled onto the ice.

The faceoff was just inside the Rangers blue line. Sniper struck hard and fast as the puck fell, snagged it, twisted around and let drive. It was a screened shot with a defenseman, big O'Brien, lunging toward him. But luck was with Bradley in goal. He didn't see the puck as it sizzled toward his net. It smacked against a goal post with a metallic clunk that could be heard throughout the arena. A long drawn "Aaah!" of relief came from the throats of the Rangers' fans.

Sniper was already racing in for the rebound. Red O'Brien loomed up and caught him with a hip. He was knocked off balance, sent staggering. Sniper recovered but Skene was already on the puck. Sniper and Skene smashed up against the boards, battling for possession. Skene whacked at the puck and sent it down the ice. Sniper raced back for it, took it off a defenseman's stick and wheeled around. Skene was after him, swept in low and threw out his stick, a quick poke check. But Sniper evaded it, leaped high over Skene's stick and broke away.

He zigzagged in on the defense, faked a pass to his left-winger and cut through the middle. Red O'Brien made a futile lunge and missed him. Sniper streaked in on goal as Leafs' fans leaped to their feet.

In he went, skates flashing. He darted across the goal crease. And then, just as he was about to unleash one of his high, hard shots, there was a moment of indecision. This goal meant everything to him. It was the most important goal of his life. It might bring victory to his team in the Cup finals. It was a huge moment in his career.

Call it nerves or stage fright or merely lack of experience in the big time. For that one fraction of a second, his concentration wavered. His confidence sagged.

When the shot left his stick, instead of the vicious, baffling backhand that had given nightmares to most goalies he faced, it was a hesitant, feeble flip that thudded into Bradley's pads. It tumbled harmlessly in front. Bradley, the relieved netminder, batted it into the corner.

A mingled howl and groan of disappointment from every Leafs' fan echoed through the huge building. They looked in vain for the red light that didn't shine.

In the broadcast booth above the ice, Foster Hewitt shouted, "Parmalee appeared to have a sure goal, but his shot was weak. Either Parmalee is suffering from the jitters or his inexperience is costing him. He made a nice rush but he didn't seem to know what to do with the puck when he was right in on goal."

Crestfallen and rattled by his failure to score when he had the tying goal on the blade of his stick, Sniper's game went to pieces. He missed a pass, then a shooting chance. Catching him with his head down, O'Brien gleefully smashed into him and sent him crashing to the ice. He crawled to the bench, dazed and bleeding from the lip but he got little sympathy from Irvin.

In the dressing room between periods, Sniper wished he could crawl into a corner and make himself invisible.

To his surprise, he found that the Leafs were not discouraged. They weren't jubilant, either, but there was no atmosphere of gloom in the room.

These men had been in the game long enough to know that much can happen in even one minute of a hockey match. The pace is so fast that games apparently lost have been turned into victories in the span of a few seconds.

Bunny sat down beside Spider. "Two periods left, old pal," he said cheerfully, slapping Sniper on the back.

"Two long periods. I'm terrible out there," said Sniper morosely. "Pathetic."

"Hey, what do you expect? You figure on skating right through some of the best hockey players in the world? Score a bunch of goals like you did in Ironwood? It's a lot tougher here. But you can play at this level. I know you can."

Sniper felt a little better. Bunny, at least, still had faith in him. But he couldn't miss some of the glances cast his way by some of the other Leafs. He knew what they were thinking. He wasn't living up to their expectations. In fact, he was an inglorious flop.

Mr. Smythe entered the room and delivered an emotional pep talk. When he left, he motioned Sniper to follow him. Sniper jumped up and huddled with the crusty manager in the corridor.

"Sniper, I have another surprise for you. I hope it'll inspire you to play your best."

Sniper was confused. "A surprise, Mr. Smythe?"

"Yes, Bunny told me about a pen pal of yours, a young lady from Wheatville."

"You mean Brenda?"

"Yep. Bunny found out that Brenda was visiting friends in Montreal this week. We tracked her down this morning and got her a train ticket and a game ticket and she's sitting right behind our bench—four rows up. She arrived just before they played the national anthem. She said to tell you she can't wait to meet you after the game."

Sniper's face lit up like a bonfire.

"I can't wait, either, Mr. Smythe. But first things first."

The moment he emerged from the corridor and stepped back on the ice, he looked up and saw her smiling face, her wave of a hand. Brenda Bates, looking lovelier than ever, was here at the game, cheering for him. He flashed her a half smile, not wanting anyone to notice, not wanting anyone to think he was not focused on the game. Of all people, she would understand why he could not be more demonstrative.

Throughout the second period, the Rangers guarded their one-goal lead, letting the Leafs carry the play to them, making sure there were always three or four players along the blue line. They looked for the charging Leafs to make a mistake, one that would pave the way to a rush down the ice and another goal.

Irvin didn't give Sniper another chance until almost midway through the period, when Leaf forwards began to wilt after the determined Rangers repulsed their attacks.

Skene beat Sniper to the draw but he didn't hold the puck long. Sniper was right on top of him, checking him so closely that Skene hurried a pass. The puck drifted off Skene's stick and

Sniper swooped after it. Once he had the puck on his stick, Sniper raced toward the Rangers' blue line, weaving in.

Butch Parmalee was waiting in his path. Scowling, he lunged out and rode Sniper hard into the boards. Sniper tried to break free, but his heavier cousin rode him cruelly into the corner and smashed him up against the screen. Sheltered there by other players who rushed in, Butch gave Sniper a bad mauling. A butt end caught him in the throat, an elbow cracked with jolting force against the side of his head. Undetected by the referee, Butch crosschecked him to the ice, and raced away with the puck. The big defenseman reached the Leafs' blue line and unleashed a shot that Bunny deflected away with his glove. A Ranger forward battled for it in the corner, sent it out in front. A wild melee followed with Bunny frantically stopping shot after shot, all from close range. Suddenly the red light flashed. A Leafs' defender, trying to clear it, had bounced the puck off Butch Parmalee's skate. It jumped back and slipped between Bunny's pads.

Rangers 2, Leafs 0.

Butch Parmalee breezed past Sniper, his arms upraised, a sneer on his face. Dabbing at a cut lip, Sniper heard his cousin's taunt. "Whatcha gonna do now, you little cow flop?"

The second period ended with the Leafs only

twenty minutes away from elimination.

Now the situation was really serious.

Sniper crouched grimly at centre. The roaring crowd had ceased to exist for him. He wasn't going to give Butch Parmalee a chance to crow for long if he could help it. That butt end to the face had aroused every bit of fight in him.

"Enjoy your lucky goal while you can, Butch," he muttered. "But don't think I'm finished yet."

He pitched in savagely at the drop of the puck, whipped it away from Skene, took half a dozen choppy strides and let drive with a shot that was high—high and fast. It sizzled straight for Butch Parmalee's head with the speed of a bullet. Butch ducked frantically, gloved hand in front of his face. He fell to his knees, one hand still covering his eyes.

"You taught me that shot," shouted Sniper. He grinned and raced through the opening, chasing after the puck.

But one of his wingers was offside and the whistle blew.

"Why all the wild shooting?" Irvin snapped when Sniper came to the bench. "Tryin' to knock Butch's head off? Next time, try a shot on goal instead."

But Sniper had achieved his goal. Butch Parmalee was boiling mad. He was wild-eyed and jittery.

Two minutes later, Sniper went out again. Skene led a rush that saw his winger dash in and drill the puck at Bunny. Bunny knocked the shot down with his stick and hurled it out to the blue line where he knew Sniper was waiting. Sniper tore away with it, his right winger racing to pull abreast. He was almost to the Rangers' blue line when he drew back his stick, faked another high shot at the crouching Butch.

Automatically, Butch threw up his arm and ducked his head. But Sniper skimmed a pass to his wing. Butch caught on too late and stumbled when he tried to react.

Sniper darted right through the defense, avoided Butch's desperate attempt to pull him down and snapped up a return pass in full flight. He flashed across the crease and cut loose with a backhand shot.

The roar of the crowd told him the puck had found the back of the net, although he knew it was labelled from the moment he sent it on it's way. Toronto fans shouted themselves hoarse.

The Rangers' lead had shrunk to one goal and there was still half a period to play.

But the Rangers weren't through by any stretch. They stormed in from the next faceoff, surging and swarming in the Leafs' zone, determined to get an insurance goal. A Leafs' defenseman panicked and drew a tripping penalty when Skene pulled away from him. Thirty seconds later, Irvin made a bad line change and his team was caught with too many men on the ice. The Leafs were two men down. It was then that Bunny Baker rose to new heights.

He resembled a target on a rifle range as pucks rained in on him. How he stopped them all was miraculous. Half a dozen times it appeared the Rangers had found a chink in his armour, but he ducked, bounced and kicked and somehow kept his net sealed.

Just when the second penalized Leaf stepped back on the ice, with time running out, Bunny golfed the puck high in the air toward centre ice. Sniper, curling under it, caught it on the blade of his stick, pushed it through Skene's legs and swept away with it. He surged in on Red O'Brien, deked around him and from thirty feet drilled the rubber on net with such force that Bradley couldn't handle it. The puck ripped into the twine and the red light flashed.

Sniper was mobbed by his teammates as Bradley slammed his goal stick against a post, shattering the blade in several pieces.

Both Bradley and Sniper glanced up at the clock. One more minute to play. The game was dead-locked and overtime appeared to be a certainty.

The Rangers called for a timeout. Sniper took a few seconds to rest and swig some water. He figured his playing time was over. But when Irvin looked down the bench at him, Sniper took a deep breath, grinned and nodded. He was ready to go.

"Get me that goal!" barked Irvin as Sniper leaped over the boards. Skene glared at him as he moved into the faceoff circle in the Rangers' zone but neither man spoke.

Skene cleverly won the draw and directed the puck to the corner boards. Sniper raced in and Skene was forced to lose precious seconds trying to break loose. Finally, he spun the puck in behind the Ranger net where Butch Parmalee was waiting. Again, Sniper wheeled and gave chase. When Butch saw him coming he couldn't resist an impulse to smash his cousin. He shot the puck around the boards and plunged into Sniper, knocking him down. Butch fell heavily on top of him, the shaft of his stick aimed at Sniper's head.

"This'll teach you," Butch snarled as he brought the stick down hard.

But Sniper rolled away and avoided the vicious check. He leaped up and slammed a shoulder into his burly cousin, and sent him reeling face first into the screen. Butch howled in pain and crashed to the ice. Blood leaked from his nose.

Sniper glanced up at the clock. Ten seconds to play. And the puck was still in the Rangers' zone. He scampered in front of the net, in time to screen Bradley from a shot that came sailing in from the blue line—high and hard. The puck rang off the cross bar and bounced out. Sniper pounced on it but Red O'Brien spun around and bodied him to the ice.

The puck lay at the end of Sniper's extended stick. The frantic roar of the crowd thundered in his ears. O'Brien moved in, hoping to snap the puck out of danger. But Sniper, with a desperate effort, got there first. One-handed, lying prone on the ice, he hooked the puck toward the net as Bradley leaped forward, intending to smother it under his glove or his pads. But when Bradley pounced, the puck wasn't there. Wood met rubber and the rubber skimmed along the ice into the open corner of the net.

A great thunderous roar greeted Sniper's goal. Sniper could hear shrieks of joy from the Leafs' fans. He also heard the buzzer signal the end of the game, but it came a split second after the red light flashed. The Leafs were Stanley Cup winners. And Sniper had delivered the winning goal!

Wisely he covered his head with both arms as his teammates pounced on him, whooping and hollering their joy. They lifted him roughly to his feet, slapped his back, shook his hand and then hoisted him onto their shoulders and paraded him around the ice. When they set him down, Bunny barrelled in and gave him a bear hug that took his breath away.

"You were great, pal," Bunny exclaimed.

"Simply great."

"No greater than you, Bunny. You won the game for us, not me."

"We both did pretty well, don't you think?" Bunny said.

"I mean, for a couple of ragamuffins who started in Wheatville and wound up on a Stanley Cup winner. How often does that happen?"

Conn Smythe, sliding out on the ice, overheard the last remark and hooted, "It never happens. But I'm glad it happened to us. It was a lucky day for the Leafs when you two rink buddies came knocking on my door."

The grim-faced Rangers waited patiently for the on-ice celebration to wind down. Then the teams lined up for the traditional handshakes. When Bunny Baker and Bradley passed each other in line, Bunny stopped and delivered another rib-crushing hug, this time to his rival.

And when Skene shook hands with Sniper, he said, "I've never played against a guy with your ability. I'll make it tough for you next year."

"You made it tough for me tonight," Sniper answered. "You're a great player, Skene."

The next Ranger in line was Butch.

Sniper hesitated, not knowing whether to extend a hand or clench a fist.

He extended his hand and Butch took it, gave it a brief shake, growled a curt, "Nice game, kid,"and moved on. We'll always be cousins but we'll never be friends, Sniper thought. There's just too much Uncle Simon in him, I guess.

Flash bulbs popped as the Leafs surrounded the Stanley Cup, which was brought onto the ice and placed on a small cloth covered table. After team captain Kelly McRae hobbled out on the ice and accepted the coveted trophy from the league president, it was cradled and caressed and kissed by the victors while flash bulbs popped and cheers continued to echo through the arena.

When the last photo was apparently taken, Conn Smythe ordered the photographer to snap one more. "Get Sniper and Bunny to pose on each side of the Cup," he barked. "I want these two rink buddies to have something to show their grand-children some day."

When the players left the ice, Sniper looked eagerly up to the fourth row. But one seat in the row was empty—Brenda's seat.

Then he heard her cry out, "Sniper, I'm here!"

She stood by the boards, near the gate, jostled by fans and players. Sniper muscled his way through the crowd and suddenly, thanks to a shove from behind by Bunny, they were close together. They threw their arms around each other, hugging, laughing, and celebrating.

And before either one even gave it a thought, their lips came together and they were kissing.

THE REST OF THE STORY

"So you had to end your story with a gooey kiss," Marty said, throwing the manuscript on the bed. "You should have ended it with Sniper giving Butch a beating at centre ice—after Butch tried to steal the Stanley Cup and run off with it."

"Too unrealistic, Marty. I think my ending is fine."

"You could have had Marty Mitchell escape from jail again. You could have had Sniper spot him in the crowd at the final game and point him out to the cops. Sniper would have been a bigger hero then."

"Again, Marty. Too unrealistic."

"O.K., but I want to know what happened next. Let's hear the rest of the story."

"But I haven't written the rest of the story."

"Well, make it up—right now. You can tell it to me. What happened to Sniper and Bunny after they won the Cup?"

"All right," Max said. "Give me a few seconds."

Marty waited patiently as his brother crossed his arms and lowered his head. He was deep in thought. Finally he looked up and said, "Here's the rest of the story. Both Sniper Parmalee and Bunny Baker enjoyed illustrious NHL careers.

Jack played for the Leafs for 12 seasons and Bunny for ten. Sniper married Brenda Bates after his second season in the NHL, the year he won the NHL scoring championship. They raised four children, two girls and two boys. In retirement, he became general manager and coach of a Junior A team in Western Canada.

"Bunny Baker married a Toronto woman, an usherette at Maple Leaf Gardens and a goaltender in women's hockey. They raised two daughters. Bunny served as a scout for the Leafs for several years and became head scout when Winky Davidson retired. Later, he became a popular commentator on Hockey Night in Canada telecasts."

"Where he often raved about the great play of the Mitchell brothers," Marty interjected. "By then Max and Marty were two of the best players in hockey."

"He might have raved about one Mitchell brother," Max said, laughing. "That would be me. Don't forget, Marty Mitchell is still in jail, serving a life sentence."

"Oh, come on. That Marty Mitchell was a fictional character. You made him up. In real life, we'll both be Leafs in a couple of years. You'll be Leaf captain and I'll be the All Star goalie."

"I'm impressed. You have a vivid imagination, brother."

"It's no bull. We're both going to be big leaguers

someday. By the way, what happened to the old coot—Uncle Simon?"

Max frowned. "Uncle Simon met a tragic end. A year after Sniper scored his famous goal, his uncle was chasing a bill collector off his property with a shotgun. He stumbled and fell on the weapon. Both barrels discharged, and...well... suffice to say his mid-section was not a pretty sight when the ambulance arrived. Parts of Uncle Simon were scattered around the barnyard. Following his death, the farm was sold and Sniper and Butch shared in the profits."

"And Conn Smythe?"

"Mr. Conn Smythe is a real person, Marty. How do I know what his future is going to be? But I'll bet he'll be a huge success in hockey. Dick Irvin and Foster Hewitt, too."

"I'm sure you're right, Max. Don't forget to send Mr. Smythe an autographed copy of your book when it's finished." Marty slapped his brother on the back—hard. "By the way, thanks again for putting my name in your book. I'll bet the kids at Merry Mabel's will soon be calling me "Killer" Mitchell. Hey, let's go down there and grab a sundae."

"Sounds good to me."

"And bring your manuscript. It's good—good enough to send to a publisher."

"No, I've got to read it over one more time. I'll

look for spelling mistakes and check the punctuation. Then I'm going to give a copy to Billy Beemer. If it wasn't for him, I'd never have written this story."

Two weeks later. Max got a note from Billy who was out of the hospital and fully recovered.

Dear Max:

That was a thrilling story you wrote for me. I enjoyed every word of it. I liked the part where you put Marty's name in the book. Now I have a confession to make. It was me who started the fire in the arena that night you saved my life. I'm sorry I lied to you. I was playing with matches in the dressing room—burning a photo of my dad that I kept in my wallet—because I was so upset with him. And I was angry because my parents were fighting all the time over his drinking. I was feeling sorry for myself because I had no real friends and I wasn't an athlete like you and Marty. I didn't care if I lived or died. I threw the burning photo of my dad in a trash can full of paper. And somehow the whole room seemed to catch fire. I didn't mean to burn the arena.

After reading your book, I said to myself, "What would Sniper do? He had a lot of problems to overcome." So I got together with my folks and told them what I really thought about our family. Now we are having lots of family talks. My dad went to

a group that deals with drinking problems and he's no longer a drunk. My folks are getting help for me from a psychiat...a mind doctor. And the best news, Max, is this. I haven't wet the bed in a long time. Your story about Sniper inspired me, Max. If Sniper can reach the top, then why can't I? I am going to take up hockey this year and I'll try to make friends with all my teammates. And I'm going to try and write some stories, too.
Your friend forever,
Billy Beemer

P.S. I promise never to play with matches again.

Max finished his novelette and sent it off to four pulp magazines. *Street & Smith's Sports Story Magazine* snapped it up, printed it in four instalments under the title Rink Buddies and paid Max 100 dollars. After he cashed the cheque, Max treated all his friends and hockey teammates to ice cream and hamburgers at Merry Mabel's. The bill came to a whopping twelve dollars. He also bought a brand new Underwood typewriter, a new pair of skates for Billy Beemer and a pearl necklace for Trudy on her birthday.